Anderson's Reinvention

A MISSION CITY GAY ROMANCE NOVELLA

GABBI GREY

Anderson

I will never regret giving up my dreams of acting to become a parent to my orphaned niece seventeen years ago. She's the light of my life, and my executive-assistant job paid for a comfortable home for us both. But now she's heading to university, and I'm facing an empty nest. Suddenly, I can focus back on who I am and what I need. And at this crossroads, who do I run into at Mission City's Christmas market but my college sweetheart. I've never forgotten Jarrod, and reconnecting brings those memories crashing back. Could there be a chance...?

Jarrod

I finished a degree in computer science, but my family needed my help back in Chilliwack. It's been a hardworking life, preserving the goat farm that was my legacy, but I kept their dream alive. After my parents passed, I threw myself into adding products like goat-milk soap, and it's been a good move. What I don't expect while working my sales booth at the Christmas market is to see Anderson wandering the aisles. He dumped me without a word seventeen years ago, and the hurt still lingers, but I admit I'm curious. Why did he run? Is he single? Within a few minutes, I realize there's a spark between us that never went out. But do I want to take any kind of chance with this man again?

Anderson's Reinvention is a second chance, interracial, opposites attract gay romance with a button-down hardworking executive assistant and the goat farmer he never forgot.

This is a work of fiction. Names, characters, places and incidents are either the products of the author's imagination, or are used fictitiously.

References to real people, events, organizations, establishments or locations are intended to provide a sense of authenticity and are used fictitiously. Any resemblance to actual events, locations, organizations, or persons living or dead is entirely coincidental.

Edits by ELF

Cover by Jo Clement

Dedication

Vanesa—because you believed we could both succeed

Contents

Chapter One

Anderson

If life were truly fair, I wouldn't have found myself sitting at my dining room table, surrounded by university pamphlets, while my daughter chatted incessantly about all her options.

My baby girl.

Well, technically my niece. From the day she'd been placed in my arms, though, I'd known I'd be responsible for taking care of her for the rest of our lives.

I'd loved my sister, and had also known caring for Adele was beyond her. Then she died in a single-car crash just three months after Adele's birth.

"I think I want to go to theater school like you did. I've done all those plays—even more than you did in high school."

"You're amazing." Easy enough to say. My daughter had talent in spades. She'd embraced every role and given it her all—even if she was merely an extra. "Still—" I bit my lip. "I want you to take something practical."

"Like business school." She rolled her eyes. "Boring." Somehow, she made the word sound as boring as the word.

"Accountants make good money."

"Dad." Again with the tone that bordered on whining.

"Adele." I could dish it back as good as she gave.

Finally, she broke. "I love theater school, but I'm going to be more practical."

Which relieved and amused me to no end. "And?"

She pulled a brochure out of the pile and handed it to me.

I blinked. "Optometry?"

She grinned. "Yep."

Completely baffled, I started to read what she'd provided me. "Three years of undergraduate science?"

"At a minimum. Even though I don't *love* school, I'd probably do four to earn my honors bachelor of science. Then, if things don't work out, I can try something else. You know, like med school or teacher's college."

My head swam. "Teacher's college is only an extra year, right?"

"Closer to two with the practicum." She snatched the brochure. "The optometry school says they don't give preference to one university over another, but I think it would be cool to go to Aunt Yvonne's alma mater. That's the University of Waterloo. And they offer the only English-language optometry school in Canada. My French isn't good enough to go to the Université de Montréal."

Her French was excellent. She had straight A-pluses in all her classes. Pretty much, she could go anywhere she wanted.

Within reason.

She handed me the brochure for an undergraduate science program at the University of Waterloo.

I did my best not to faint. *You priced out universities closer to home, and they're not much cheaper.* The university in Abbotsford was the closest and the most logical. Except it didn't rival the University of British Columbia or, apparently, the University of Waterloo.

"Aunt Yvonne said if I get in, she'll pay the tuition, books, and residence costs."

"What?" I tried to wrap my mind around what a gift that would be. I'd been saving for Adele's university fund as soon as I'd been able. Thinking about all the times I'd gone out for drinks with friends, or on hookups that required hotel rooms, or... I slammed the door shut. I was not going to feel guilty about trying to have a life beyond my beloved child. I cleared my throat. "I'll have to talk to Yvonne. That would mean—" I gulped.

Adele placed her hand over mine. "I know."

I blinked. "Yvonne isn't—"

"Blood? Yeah, I know. But she says she wants me to have the same opportunities as Paget and Sedona—even though they're her real family."

"They're all our family." My boss, Shaw, had met Damien in...interesting circumstances. Damien had brought his twin daughters into the relationship. Along for the ride was his sister-in-law, Yvonne. Damien hadn't coped with the death of his wife very well—because who would? In the end, he'd accepted his sister-in-law's help.

"How does Yvonne have all this money?"

Adele shrugged. "The life insurance money from the twins' mom's death is going to pay for their schooling. Yvonne...I dunno. She's had really important jobs and done really amazing things. Apparently, she'd just been saving that money. Now she wants me to have it."

I cleared my throat again. "I'll need to have a chat with her. I guess you need to start filling out these applications shortly?"

She bit her lower lip.

"Ah, you've already filled them out. You just wanted to prepare me if these institutions come back with acceptances."

She hopped out of her seat, pecked a kiss on my cheek, and headed upstairs to her room.

I slowly began to collect all the brochures, ensuring the one for the University of Waterloo was on top. *Should've agreed to theater school.* In the next heartbeat, the idea of my daughter becoming an optometrist warmed my heart. What I needed to do was contact Yvonne. Her offer was way too generous. I looked around the house I'd finished paying for just two years ago. My mother's unexpected passing had left a life insurance policy that paid the mortgage and put a small amount aside for Adele's schooling. I didn't regret not having made the mortgage payments for this time, but should I have put all the money into an account for Adele? I just didn't know.

A knock sounded at my door.

I frowned.

Adele thundered down the stairs. "Uncle Damien's here."

"Uh, okay."

At the foot of the stairs, she turned to stare. "You're going to the Christmas Market with him while I'm going to see the movie with Sedona and Paget." She held out her hands.

I dug in my pocket and pulled out my keys.

She kissed me on the cheek, then headed to the front door. She swung it open with a huge grin. "Hi, Uncle Damien."

"Hello, kiddo. Drive safe, okay?"

Through the open doorway, I spotted his daughters leaning against my car. To my relief, his was parked next to it.

As Adele bounced down the driveway, Damien stepped into the hallway and shut the door. "You're just glad I didn't bring the motorcycle."

"Would've been tough to ride with two grown daughters on the back." I snagged my jacket. "Sorry, I forgot."

"What's up?"

"Adele is talking universities, and I'm seeing dollar signs."

Damien nodded. "I have some saved for the girls. Plus, there's the life insurance from their mom's policy. Shaw, of course, has already made it clear he'll pay whatever."

I nudged Damien as we headed out the door. "Guess it's good to be married to some rich guy."

His blue eyes sparkled in the bright December daylight. "Would've chosen him if he had nothing. Him saving my life kind of sealed the deal, though."

So much said and unsaid. Their story was far more complicated than just Shaw saving Damien after he was swept away by a rockslide and nearly thrown down the embankment and into the Fraser River.

No, Shaw had helped Damien cope with his grief and, in the end, assisted him in finding the strength to reunite with his daughters.

Daughters who easily accepted Shaw, and his dog Rufus, into their lives. Everyone was ready for a fresh start, and Mission City had offered that to them.

Including Yvonne.

I hopped into Damien's SUV.

He got in as well and hit the heater. "I can't believe how cold it is out there."

"December tends to be chilly. Although January and February are worse, and you, my friend, should know that by now."

"There's nothing like Thunder Bay cold." He backed out of my driveway. "But I've come to expect warmer."

I chuckled. "Well, it's British Columbia. Wait ten minutes, and the weather will change." I considered. "Why are we the ones going to the Christmas Market?"

He chuckled right back. "Because we're exchanging homemade gifts this year. Shaw is taking the girls to the Richmond Night Market next weekend. Since everything is supposed to be a surprise, I figured we'd do this market. Biggest one in Mission City all year."

"Really?" I shook my head as he pulled into the parking lot.

And nabbed a spot near the back of what appeared to be a completely full lot.

"Nice job."

"The high school's parking lot is available as well. We just got lucky." He brushed his lapel, as if buffing his nails, in self-satisfaction.

I laughed, loving his smile. And the flecks of silver in his goatee were far more pronounced than when we'd met four years ago.

God, four years.

Time had flown past as we'd watched our daughters grow. Adele was a year older than Paget and Sedona—and had always been far more mature.

I'd worried she might be a bad influence—she wasn't an angel—but she took her role as pseudo big sister seriously.

We hopped out of the SUV and headed toward the rec center. I'd spent countless hours here watching Adele during her swim lessons. She'd even tried figure skating for a year. Nothing had stuck, and she much preferred video games. Since I wasn't happy with that, the compromise was she would play recreational badminton. Understanding that playing with me would be *uncool*, I let her join a league of people I mostly knew from around town. An architect, a dentist, an elementary school teacher, amongst others. She tolerated my watching.

Barely.

I hunched my shoulders against the bitter wind. "How can it be so sunny and so freaking cold?"

Damien chuckled. "Try a northern Ontario winter."

"Weren't you just complaining about the cold?" I chuckled, then nodded gratefully as the person at the door held it open for us. "Hey, Blake, thanks."

They smiled. "Hope to see you at Starbucks later. I'll have your favorite latté waiting." They glanced up at Damien. "Your coffee will be fresh."

Damien grinned. "You're too good to me."

With that, we went our separate ways.

I was so reassured to see Blake happy. They'd struggled in recent years—without family support through their transition. Working at the local coffee shop, with a hugely supportive staff who felt like family, had made it easier for them. Well, as easy as life could be, given the cards they'd been dealt.

A jovial woman in a Santa cap was happy to take our admittance fee and to stamp our hands.

"Thank you."

"Oh, my pleasure. Good cause."

Damien and I stepped toward the hall. I gazed up at him. "Do you know which cause we're supporting?"

"Does it matter?" He unzipped his coat. "Damn, I didn't bring cloth shopping bags."

"Oof. Neither did I. I suppose we could buy some."

He winced. "I already have so many—" He considered. "—in the back of my SUV."

I waved him off. "Go."

"I'll grab a couple for you as well."

"That'll be lovely." I eyed the first stall. "I'll wait."

"Awesome." He tapped my shoulder. "Be right back."

After he took off, I attempted to survey the room. I was shorter than he was. Hell, I was now shorter than my daughter. I liked to think I made up for my height deficiency with my robust and oversized personality.

You mean oversized ego.

I rolled my eyes at my inner voice. In truth, I tried to be confident without being cocky—no small feat.

As my gaze roamed the various stalls, I saw my Ghost of Christmas Past.

Chapter Two

Jarrod

Holy fucking shit.

Like crap on a cracker.

Stay calm, for fuck's sake.

He might not even recognize you

Even though you sure as shit recognize him.

I smiled at the lovely woman before me with her long auburn hair and her lovely brown eyes. Her husband stood just behind her.

Like me, he was a big guy—tall, muscular, and fit. His dark skin matched my own, only where my smile was now forced, his appeared genuine. He touched his wife's shoulder.

Well, I assumed wife. They wore matching wedding bands, after all. She'd introduced herself as *Loriana, the librarian,* and the gentleman as *Mitch*.

"What are you thinking?" He gave her a dazzling smile.

"I'm thinking soap for everyone at the library, including Miss Edna."

"Yes, we can't forget Miss Edna," said with clear affection.

"Do you think the male-identifying volunteers would like them?" She picked one up and sniffed it. Her eyes glazed with bliss. "Oh, and I would need to take one to make certain." She held the lavender soap in her hand.

Crap. Is she going to take that home and only come back if she likes it? All my scents were amazing. My goat's milk soaps were popular year-round, but I made the most money working Christmas markets up and down Cedar Valley as well as a few in the suburbs of Vancouver. Tables were expensive, though, so I had to watch how many I secured.

My first love stepped closer.

The woman turned to him. "Hey, Anderson, great to see you."

"Lovely to see you too, Loriana." He pivoted his attention to the much-taller gentleman. "Mitch."

The height difference between the men was pronounced. But then, Anderson had always been on the short side. Hell, Loriana was a couple of inches taller than him.

"Okay, man's opinion." She held a bar of vanilla soap to his nose.

He inhaled deeply and shut his eyes in obvious ecstasy. "Oh yeah, I'd buy all of them." He opened his dark-brown eyes, and that powerful gaze settled on me.

Okay, he totally remembers.

"That's the vanilla scent." I gestured to my table. "I have twelve different scents..." I just couldn't pull out the sales pitch I normally used.

Loriana nodded, gazing intently at Anderson. "Would you want to receive one of these?"

"As a gift? I'd be thrilled." He leaned closer. "And not just because I'm a gay man who loves his skin routines."

Mitch chuckled. "As a straight man, I say the gift is pretty awesome as well. I like that the scent is subtle. Likely won't trigger a migraine for anyone with scent allergies."

Lorianna grinned. "You're brilliant."

"Uh, I try."

Without an iota of doubt, I was certain the man was blushing. With his dark skin, though, the flush wasn't visible.

"Okay." Loriana furrowed her brow. "That's Marnie, Johanna..." She started counting on her fingers. "Oh, might as well make it twenty."

"Because any leftovers will definitely be put to good use." Mitch kissed her cheek. "I'd be happy to find one under my tree."

Her lovely eyes lit. "Oh. I love it when you're direct." She turned her attention back to me. "Two of each and three of the lavender."

"I have twelve scents—" *She said twenty...right?*

She waved me off. "I am certain I can find more people to share with. A couple of the patrons are lonely this time of year."

"Well, if you buy a dozen, you get one free." Since I rarely sold a dozen at a time, I didn't have to worry about that often. The offer was on the sign, but most people either didn't see it or didn't feel inclined to take me up on that.

"Okay. I'll take these two. One lavender and one..." She eyed Anderson. "Lemon?"

"He'd prefer vanilla." I cleared my throat.

Three people turned to me with varying quizzical looks.

Loriana's gaze shot back and forth between Anderson and me. "Well, that's interesting. And if I didn't have tons of shopping left to do, I might consider demanding to know stuff that you might not want to share."

Mitch chuckled. "Watch out. She considers herself the matchmaking queen of Mission City."

My eyes widened, but Anderson's glittered. "Yes, all those successes."

Loriana pouted. "I try."

Mitch kissed her cheek. "We know you do." He turned his attention to me. "Twenty-four with a bonus lavender for my wife and vanilla for our friend." He pivoted to Anderson. "If you don't mind Loriana's...interference."

His smile turned a little bashful. "Yeah, that would be okay."

I took the cloth bag Mitch handed me and put the twenty-five bars of soap in it. I handed the vanilla to Loriana.

She grinned. Then pivoted and handed it to Anderson. "I want credit for this later."

"Credit for what?" A tall, handsome older gentleman with piercing blue eyes approached. He nudged Anderson. "What'd I miss? Nice to see you, Loriana. Mitch."

"Oh, Damien. Nice to see you too. How's your husband, Shaw?"

No missing the emphasis on *husband*. Just in case I needed to know, Anderson was single. How the hell no one had snapped him up in the last seventeen years was beyond me—but here he was, evidently on his own.

"Do you take credit cards?" Mitch handed me one.

"Yeah, thanks." I calculated the transaction, entered the amount into the card reader, and let Mitch tap. Once I had the confirmation, I handed him the receipt. "My farm address is on there. I'm just over in Chilliwack. If anything's not to your liking, I offer a full refund."

Mitch gripped the bag. "I seriously doubt that'll be an issue."

Loriana presented the bar of soap to Anderson. "Later."

He grinned and accepted the gift.

Within a moment, the couple were gone.

Leaving me face-to-face with the love of my life and the guy who was apparently...his friend?

I cleared my throat. "Nice to see you again." Because clearly my knowing his favorite scent was vanilla—and him not arguing—meant I remembered him.

He offered a soft smile. "And you." He turned to his friend. "Damien, this is Jarrod. We went to college together. I was studying theater, and he was studying IT." He turned back to me, the question clear in his eyes.

How did you go from studying IT in Vancouver to selling goat's milk soap at a Christmas Market in Mission City and running a goat farm in Chilliwack?

Since I knew nothing about what had happened to him in the intervening years for him, I didn't ask. Instead, I smiled. "My family convinced me to return to the farm. I do some computer stuff on the side, but my focus is the goat farm." I gestured. "And making goat-milk products."

Damien stepped forward to grasp the lemon-zing scented soap.

"Good for a wake-me-up in the morning." I offered my salesperson smile.

He grinned back. "My daughter Paget could use this. She's hard to wake." He pivoted to Anderson. "You know, this would really be good for Adele."

"Adele?" Because I was too damn curious for my own good.

Anderson met my gaze. "My daughter."

He had a... My brain stuttered. Then shifted back into gear. Of course, he had a daughter. The world hadn't stayed suspended for seventeen years.

Well, for one of us, anyway.

"She's actually my niece. But I adopted her a few months after her mother, my sister, died. I consider her my own in every way that matters."

"I see." Because I did. That was exactly something Anderson might do. "Uh, how old is she? You said her name was Adele?"

He nodded. "She's seventeen." His gaze held mine.

"How old was she when her mother died?" An incredibly personal question, but an image was forming in my mind. A notion too painful to contemplate.

"Three months. I lost my sister almost two decades ago." He swallowed. "That kind of pain never leaves, you know?" He turned to his friend. "Sorry, I wasn't thinking. I didn't mean—"

Damien placed his hand on Anderson's chest. "I miss my wife every day. That loss will, as you say, never leave. But I found a way to move on. A great husband, his friends—" He tapped Anderson's nose. A rather intimate gesture for two men who were *just friends*.

But then, who was I to judge? I had no close friends.

Anderson pivoted back to me. "Three lemon zings and two more vanilla. Where in Chilliwack?" He asked the question casually as he pulled out his wallet.

If I hadn't needed the money, I would've given them to him for free.

"Is it okay if I give them as gifts?" Anderson met Damien's gaze. "Oh, better make it four of each. I almost forgot Shaw's housekeeper."

Damien laughed. "Oh, she'll be tickled you remembered her. Yes, it's fine you're giving these as gifts. I'm certain I can find something else. Too bad you've already got one for yourself—I could have bought it for you."

"He loves homemade maple fudge." I wrote out a receipt for Anderson. Then I collected the soaps and put them in the bag he held. The one Damien had given him earlier.

"Homemade maple fudge." Damien licked his lips. "I doubt it'd survive until Christmas because that sounds decadent."

"You can buy some for yourself and some for Anderson." My friend Shea made the stuff, and the concoction was truly divine. I had to resist walking past her table because I could easily spend all my profits on her treats. Which was good neither for my bottom line, not my waistline. I didn't want to worry about these things. At thirty-nine, though, I was starting to realize time wasn't on my side. *Right.* I entered the amount in the card reader.

Anderson tapped his card. "Where in Chilliwack?"

I swallowed as I handed him the receipt.

He met my gaze.

"Uh, near Chilliwack Mountain Road."

"I'm going to head over to the fudge stand. If I buy enough to satisfy myself, then I can get some for you as well." Damien rubbed his flat stomach. "I'm liking this homemade-gift thing."

"Yeah." Anderson continued to hold my gaze.

"Oh, there's a guy who sells the most amazing pumpkin pies. And another guy who sells sparkling apple cider." I considered. "You said you have daughters?"

"Three between the two of us." Damien grinned. "Making me grayer by the minute." His eyes showed real warmth and affection.

"Well, my friend Henry makes glass fairy figurines. They're...unique. Maybe not for older teenagers, though."

"We're looking for unique gifts. Not everything has to be practical." His grin turned pensive. "Our girls have just about anything they could need—they're really lucky. We all are. That's one of the reasons we're going with handmade this year. Well, handmade by someone. We wanted to focus on the act of giving rather than the amount being spent. Your soaps are perfect." He turned to Anderson. "I'll meet up with you in a bit. I'm going to try to keep the other gifts a secret, and you're the worst secret keeper ever."

No, he's not. He kept my secret all those years ago. Has likely kept them all this time—if he's even thought about me.

Anderson grinned unrepentantly. "Is it my fault everyone comes to me?"

Damien's laugh lines showed when he guffawed. "Oh, it's good to see some things never change. You'll survive Adele going to university. I'll hate it if Paget or Sedona—or both—choose to move away. But I'll survive." He turned back to me. "Fairies, eh? I like the sound of that. You two get caught up." He left.

And I wanted to speak to Anderson—if I could even find the words—but a line had formed, and I really needed the money.

As if understanding, he stood to the side.

Customer after customer came.

Still, he stayed close.

I thought I was about to get a breather when a woman with striking white-blonde hair and the most exquisite eyes I'd ever seen stepped forward. I'd have called them amber. They were definitely unique.

"Okay." She grinned. "My friend Loriana told me about you, and I just have to grab a few bars. I promised something unique for my friends Tarah and Allie and they're just going to die over these. So, uh, five? One lavender and you can pick the other scents."

I couldn't figure out how she went from naming two friends and came out with five, but I certainly wasn't going to complain.

As I rang her up, she noticed Anderson. "Sheesh. You're quiet. I find that a change." She winked.

He grinned back.

She snapped her fingers. "Clay's going to sell out of his pumpkin spice again this year if you don't race over there. Felicia loves it."

"How do you know what spices Shaw's housekeeper uses?" He arched an eyebrow.

"Because she was talking to Remy at the grocery store and lamenting the lack of spice selection. Remy bought some of the pumpkin spice here last year." Her brow furrowed. "Or at least I think that's the order. Anyway, you know how this town is. Someone told me that they told Felicia, and that person suggested to me that it would make a good gift. I'm not close enough to Shaw or Damien to make the suggestion—"

I blinked. Chilliwack was about three times larger than Mission City, but I couldn't fathom everyone here knew everyone else.

"Rielle, you're a sweetheart." Anderson squeezed her arm. "Yes, I'll run over to see Clay. Do you know if Ashton's with him?"

Rielle rolled her eyes. "Where you find one..."

"Right." He pivoted his gaze to me. "I'll be back. I promise."

We'll see. You said that once before...

Chapter Three

Anderson

"I'm down to my last fifteen jars." Clay grinned. His eyes sparkled with pleasure, and his reddish-auburn hair shone in the light.

"I told him he didn't make enough." That husbandly pride couldn't be overstated. Ashton's grin outshone Clay's.

"Well, the Autumn Market is usually where I do the most business. I almost didn't take a table here—"

"Would've been a huge mistake." Ashton grinned.

"Not going to argue with that."

I laughed. "No, arguing with one's husband is never a good idea." I eyed the jars. "I'll take two. I don't want to empty your table."

"It's so good." Ashton pressed his hand against his belly. "You have no idea."

Clay nudged him. "Why don't you give him a taste? I saved a couple of cookies for special customers."

"Oh, I can't." I was a guaranteed sale. Better to keep them for people who were hedging.

Ashton waved me off as he grabbed a container from under the desk. "You can have mine. I can always bake more." He held out the tin which had a few remaining.

Not wanting to be rude, I snagged one. "Thank you." Then I bit into the pumpkin-spice cookie. My eyes widened. After chewing, I swallowed. "I think I've died and gone to heaven."

Clay laughed as he handed me a brochure. "Several recipes as well as my website where you can find more. I'm always looking for new ones."

"I'll buy two more jars." I eyed the cookies.

"I can wrap another cookie for you. If there's someone special you want to share it with." Even as Ashton said the words, a little blush stole across his cheeks.

"That would be awesome. He...won't be expecting this." *Should I give Jarrod a jar as well? What if he doesn't bake? Well, there must be someone in this life.* That thought gave me pause. No way, after seventeen years, was sweet and loveable Jarrod still single. That just didn't happen. Guys like him were snapped up. *Unlike guys you might resemble? You're single. Or did you forget that little fact?*

"Are you okay?" Ashton handed me a cookie in a paper sleeve with Clay's logo emblazoned on it.

"Good marketing." I gestured.

"Well, I do have a business degree with a specialization in marketing. I still work for Noel Barker, but only part-time." Clay gestured to his last few jars of spice. "This keeps me busy."

"Not enough for full-time?" I was curious.

"With Ashton helping? Not quite. I don't like to be idle, and Noel was great, giving me a job right out of university. Maybe one day this will be all I do, but I like to keep my fingers in several pies. Oh, speaking of pies—have you tried Wyatt's mom's pumpkin pie? She uses my spices for some of her recipes, and I have to say they're divine."

"I'll head over that way."

"Better hustle—they're as popular as my stuff." Clay waved. "Nice to see you again."

I had more than a decade on the two men, but their friendliness always made me smile. Well, Ashton was a touch shyer, but he'd been coming into his own after meeting, and now marrying, Clay. "Yeah, thanks."

Finding Wyatt's table was easy. He and Tate were swamped.

I stood in line, waiting my turn, when Wyatt's mother appeared with a baby stroller. Unless she'd made an interesting life choice, the baby must belong to the couple.

A couple who'd had their own struggles. High school sweethearts, separated when Tate went to school in Toronto, moved to London, England, and then wound up back in Mission City. He and Wyatt reconnected, and they now lived at Wyatt's family's pumpkin farm. "Hey Mrs. Phelps—I see you've got some precious cargo."

She grinned the grin of a satisfied grandmother. "Born six weeks ago. Tate's sister Tamlyn offered to be a surrogate for the boys."

"Oh, wow. That's a huge commitment."

"I know, right? But she saw how happy they were together and knew they really wanted a family of their own. I keep offering to move out—"

"Thank God she hasn't." Tate appeared, kissed his mother-in-law on the cheek, and gazed down at his daughter. "How's she been?"

"Coralie's been an angel. I've fed, changed, and cuddled her. She's passed out."

"Undoubtedly from all that love." I smiled. "I remember when Adele was that age." I met Tate's gaze. "They grow up so freaking fast. Watch out."

"We're going to treasure every minute, I promise." He turned to his mother-in-law. "Do you want me to watch her?"

"Would you? I found something I want to buy. Then I'll come back and help you clean up. I'm so pleased to see you sold all the pies."

Dismayed, I turned to find that, indeed, all the pies were sold and Wyatt was starting to fold the tablecloth.

No doubt Tate caught my dismayed expression. He leaned over. "For you, Anderson? When the disappointed crowd is gone, we'll give you one of the couple we save for special friends."

I blinked. I knew Wyatt and Tate. Had gone to school with Tate's brother, William. But to receive such a generous offer? "Oh, I couldn't—"

Mrs. Phelps put her hand on my arm. "I'd be ever so pleased if you did. Truly."

"Well, who am I to turn down such a generous offer? I need to find—"

Even as I said the words, Damien sauntered over. "Those glass fairies are stunning. Several are LGBTQ. I bought one for Paget that I know she's going to love. She might not be into girly things, but this...?"

"I should run and get one for Adele so she doesn't feel left out."

"Already taken care of. But she's getting it from her Uncle Damien and Uncle Shaw. We're totally taking credit for this one."

"That's fair." I smiled as Wyatt surreptitiously handed me a pie.

He grinned. "My mom's amazing. Baking all these pies *and* helping to take care of Coralie." His blue eyes sparkled. "Helps that Tate's on parental leave from his job at the bank, but it's still a lot. Who knew bok choy would be so popular?" The pumpkin farm also contained numerous greenhouses where they grew the popular vegetable.

"People who are healthy?" Damien grinned.

"Oh, are you ready to go? I want to go back to the soap booth." I aimed for casual.

He eyed me speculatively.

"Jarrod?" Mrs. Phelps grinned. "I stock up every time I see him—quality product at a reasonable price. Young man's always so busy."

I had to remind myself that Wyatt and Tate were just a couple of years younger than myself and Mrs. Phelps likely saw them as her *boys* as well. Sometimes we always remained young in the eyes of our parents.

Adele's never growing old. She'll always be my baby girl.

"Yes, Jarrod. I bought a few soaps as gifts." I pivoted to Damien. "Ten minutes?"

"Sure." His gaze narrowed.

I shrugged and headed back to my old *friend.*

To find him packing up his booth. He had several wood crates, and he was putting up the stands he'd used to display his wares.

"How'd you do?"

He glanced up, his startled gaze meeting my hopeful one. He cleared his throat. "Sold out. That's never happened. Thank you."

"I doubt my sales made the difference."

"You're wrong. I sold my last bar five minutes ago. If you hadn't bought yours, then I would've had a few left over. That's not a big deal, but it's exciting to sell out."

"I'll bet. Do you need a hand?" I moved to put my bags on the cleared part of his table, but he held up his hand. "I've got this part down to an art. Or a science. Or...whatever." He swallowed.

Okay...so not indifferent. "Do you think—" This time, I swallowed.

"Yeah?" His eyes brightened.

"Do you need to get back to the farm? Are the goats okay?"

"It's sweet you're thinking of them. They'll be okay for a while. I have a young woman from a neighboring farm who helps out. She checked on them an hour ago and texted they were fine."

I nodded. "Well then...Fifties?"

He grinned. "Greasy diner?"

"My treat."

His grin faltered a little. "I can pay my own way."

"No one said you couldn't—but I'm asking and you're accepting. You can pick up the tab the next time." *Next time? Isn't that a little overoptimistic? You haven't even had one—*

"Is this a date?"

I startled at his use of the word I had in my mind. "Do you want it to be?" I peered at him—willing him to accept.

His smile was wide and toothy. "Yeah, I think it might just be."

I was about to respond when Damien sidled up to me. "You ready to go?"

"Uh—"

"You two came together?" Jarrod waved his hand between the two of us.

"I drove him, yeah." Damien cocked his head. "Our daughters went to the movies together in his car. I didn't feel like making him walk."

Jarrod smiled. "So you're a good friend?"

I gazed into Damien's eyes, willing him to understand.

"Best of friends. I met him through his boss—my husband—but Anderson's incredibly special to me and my daughters. We had it rough for a bit, but he helped smooth things out." He offered me a wistful smile, then pivoted his attention back to Jarrod. "So yes, we're friends."

"Well, that's great. He asked me to go to Fifties with him for dinner. Are you coming?"

For one panicked moment, I thought Damien might agree. Then I walked back the panic. He was a friend. He could be my wingman. Still, I waited to hear his answer.

He shook his head. "Lovely offer. My husband's been minding my crockpot today. Anderson's daughter Adele and my twins are all going to be home soon. We're planning a big meal and then a sleepover."

First, I'd heard of the sleepover. They weren't uncommon—what with Adele being as much older sister as friend to Damien's two.

He gave me *that* look.

I nearly rolled my eyes.

He was clearing the decks for me, so to speak. Ensuring I had the house to myself should I wish a...gentleman caller.

My house was inherited from my mother. In all the years I'd lived there, I'd never once—not a single solitary time—brought a guy home.

Yet, in a heartbeat, I knew I could bring Jarrod home. "That's kind of you."

"There's some new streaming thingy that dropped on Monday and the girls have been dying to see it. I figure a little more screen time—and maybe some extra popcorn—will be okay. We're so close to the Christmas break anyway." He gestured to my bag of gifts. "Want me to hide those?"

He had keys to my house and would be there to greet the girls anyway, so him taking them made sense. "Yeah, that would be great." I arched an eyebrow. "Do *not* sample the pie."

"You got pie?"

I laughed. “Mrs. Phelps has a soft spot for me. I got one from her special stash.”

“You'll have to share your secret later.” He carefully took my bags. “Behave.” Before I could respond, he turned to Jarrod. “Take care of him, eh? He's one of the good ones.”

Jarrod met my gaze, then turned to Damien. “I intend to. I know how special Anderson is.”

Chapter Four

Jarrod

I know how special Anderson is.

I replayed the words in my head as I drove us the mile to Fifties. The diner sat on the main street in Mission City—a true relic of the past. I'd met friends here for dinner a few times over the years—always hoping to run into Anderson but it never happening.

In truth, I hadn't been certain he'd come back to Mission City after leaving college.

One day we'd been in love and planning our lives together.

The next he'd been gone without a word.

I never knew what had happened. Why he'd just been gone in the blink of an eye. At the time, I considered trying to track him down. Had even put his name in a search engine.

But I could never bring myself to clicking on the magnifying glass. I had mad programming skills—so I could've totally done the search without raising any suspicions. I hadn't, though. No one mentioned him going missing, so I figured he had good reasons to fuck off and not tell me why or where he was going.

Might I discover those reasons tonight?

Not likely. And I wasn't going to ask. If he volunteered the information, I'd certainly listen. If not, I'd be content to just bask in the pleasantness of being in his company.

Seventeen years was a long time.

Certainly long enough to heal a broken heart.

Right?

"I haven't been here in ages." I cut the engine and unbuckled my seatbelt.

"Adele loves coming here for the milkshakes. I think I'm here once a month. Damien and Shaw take their tuns as well. Our girls really are inseparable. I don't know what's going to happen when Adele goes to university next autumn." He blinked. "But it's cold out here. Let's go inside. Hopefully we can get a table."

We were at almost six o'clock—likely a busy time for the diner. "If the line's too long, there are about a dozen other places we can go." Some were fast food, and some were over in Abbotsford, but I didn't care. Anything to spend more time with this amazing man.

He grinned. "Yeah, we'll figure something out."

Within moments, we were out of my pickup truck and hustling over to the restaurant. We made it inside, and I was assailed with the smell of grease, French fries, and something I couldn't quite identify. Whatever the scent was, I wanted some of that.

A curvy blonde with sparkling-blue eyes greeted us. "Hey, Anderson." She pivoted to me. "And Anderson's friend."

Anderson slid his arm around my waist and tucked himself into my side.

Like he always used to do.

"This is Jarrod. He's my date." He gazed up at me. "Jarrod, this is Sarabeth. She's the heart and soul of this place."

She laughed. "More like a lowly servant." She winked. "I love my job. Because I love people." She tapped Anderson's chest with her pen. "You're always big on flattery."

"I call it like I see it."

"Well, Carter and Byron just settled up their tab and are leaving. If you give me thirty seconds to clear the booth, it's all yours."

"Fantastic." Anderson waved at two men headed our way. "Carter, the younger one, is a fantasy writer. Byron is an accountant." He said the words quietly—clearly, so I'd be the only one to hear them. He put on a wide smile as the men approached.

I had to admit, they made an interesting pair.

Byron was likely in his forties. A little stiff and formal.

Carter, whose skin was about my color, sauntered with a bit of swagger—but not in a bad way. Just a guy who appeared really happy. He stuck out his hand. "Anderson, great to see you again."

Anderson grinned. "Nice to see you too. So glad your book came out last month. We've all read it."

"I appreciate that."

"And the girls are thrilled they all own signed copies."

He ducked his head. "Well, nice of Dickens to host a signing for me at The Owl's Nest." Then he straightened. "The next book in the series is finished and on my editor's desk."

Anderson's eyebrows shot up. "So soon?"

Carter chuckled. "Remember that it takes over a year from submission to publication. The book you just read? I finished writing it almost two years ago. I feel like I'm slower these days." He pecked Byron's cheek. "Probably because I love spending time with my husband and our two pups."

"Ah yes, how are Sheffield and Rosebud?"

Byron, whose cheeks were still a little pink after Carter's kiss, offered a shy smile. "Both doing exceedingly well. Just happy dogs. Helps they have two dads who spoil them."

Carter laughed. "I love being a dad." He paused. "Oh, how could I forget? We're fostering a rescue dog right now. Her name's Mei. She's the cutest thing. Looking for a forever home." He batted his eyelashes at Anderson.

He laughed. "Not right now. Adele's heading to university, and I'm looking at having the house to myself for the first time ever. I'm not certain I want to be tied down with the responsibility of a dog."

"That's fair. The brood are with my family. Rosebud is Tansy's favorite." He pivoted to me. "My sister."

"Ah." I bit back the question on the tip of my tongue. *Are you going to have children?* That question always popped into my head when I met a gay couple who didn't have kids. Probably because I wanted them so badly myself.

"I had considered getting a dog." Anderson shrugged. "Between Adele, and Shaw's dog Rufus, I've got enough chaos in my life."

"The shepherd, right? Doesn't he shed everywhere?" Byron tilted his head.

"Yep." Anderson grinned. "And he's Shaw's problem. The last time he and Damien snuck away, Adele and I went to stay at their house. So although my clothes came home covered in dog hair, I didn't actually have to worry about my house."

Right. Well, he's not going to want to be around a guy who works in barns and deals with goat shit.

"Anderson? Jarrod? Your booth is ready. Last one on the left-hand side."

Anderson blinked. "Oh God, I haven't even introduced you. Carter, Byron, this is my old friend Jarrod. Well, he's not old. I mean not as old as—" He winced.

Byron chuckled. "I'm not *that* much older than the two of you. Nothing like the age difference with my husband."

Carter beamed. "And yet he still puts up with me."

"I'm the lucky one." Even below the music, Byron's words were clear. "We'll leave you to your dinner. Jarrod, I hope to see you around again. Anderson needs more friends." He cleared his throat.

Carter grinned, threading his arm through his husband's. "Night."

They escaped through the door, and a blast of cold air blew through.

Anderson shivered. "Let's get to the booth where it'll be much warmer."

As predicted, the booth—at the back of the restaurant—was much warmer. I wanted to tuck him beside me, but decorum dictated we sit across from each other. The booth would've been a tight fit with the two of us next to each other.

We shed our coats, and each grabbed a menu.

"Are you going to have a milkshake?" I waited for him to gaze up from the menu.

He did.

Our gazes met. His eyes were the same shade of light brown that I remembered. Eyes that haunted my dreams and fed my waking fantasies. I'd never met anyone with that exact shade.

"Don't you think it's a little chilly?" He pretended to shiver. "I was thinking maybe a coffee with dinner or a hot chocolate with dessert."

"Coffee? This late?"

He frowned. "It's only six. On a Saturday night."

"Oh." Right. Because he didn't have to get up at some ungodly hour to take care of the goats.

"But you have a point about caffeine. I live on the stuff. Adele is a night owl, and I do my best to be in the office before Shaw most days. I always manage to get some sleep, but I do enjoy my weekend mornings when I get to sleep in." He eyed me. "I suppose you don't get to sleep in on the farm?"

"Nah, not really. But I always was an early bird." Which was true. He'd been what I termed a *normal* person—up at a reasonable hour and to bed the same. Unless he was doing a theater production. Then he was at the theater till all hours of the night rehearsing and then show times.

I'd never missed a performance. Not a single one.

He'd walked away from all that. Now I knew why.

"What can I get you guys?" Sarabeth put two glasses of water before us.

I hadn't even looked at the menu. I gestured for Anderson to go first.

"Okay, I have to try the Blue Moon shake. Adele's going to lose her mind if it's as good as it looks."

Sarabeth grinned. "Even better. You getting something to eat?"

"I'll have the spicy Cajun chicken burger. Side of Caesar."

"Great." She pivoted to me.

"I'll have the classic cherry milkshake."

"Oh, good choice." Anderson grinned. "One of my favorites."

Sarabeth chuckled. "You love all of them."

"Hey, black licorice is disgusting."

My eyebrows shot up. "Black licorice. Oh, I love—"

"No goodnight kiss if you do that. I mean, gross." He screwed up his face. Then, as if realizing what he'd just said, his cheeks turned an interesting shade of pink.

"Cherry it is." Sarabeth tried to hide a smile—and totally failed. "Dinner?"

"Well, a little odd, but can I get the mushroom and cheese omelet?"

"Sure." She cocked her head. "Why odd?"

"Well, an omelet for dinner."

"Honey, one of my favorite customers orders meatloaf for breakfast. We're open twenty-four hours, and you never know what they've just done when someone arrives. For all I know, you work the night shift and this is your breakfast." She snagged the menus. "Anything else?"

We shook our heads.

"But I reserve the right to order dessert." Anderson spoke to Sarabeth, but his gaze was on me. "Possibly to share."

"Chocolate lava cake?"

His gaze shot to the server. "You know me too well."

"You were coming in here long before I started working. I'll save you one." With that, she took off.

"That long?" I sipped my water.

"My mom brought me here when I was a kid. I mean, it's been around since the fifties. Her favorite place to come."

"How is she doing?"

He cleared his throat. "She died two years ago."

"Oh shit." I winced. "I always was good at stepping in it."

He waved me off. "You didn't have any way of knowing. Cancer. She was gone way too soon. Still had some living to do." He sipped his water. "I'm sorry Adele had to watch her grandmother suffer, but that matured her. I would've tried to shield her, but she didn't want any part of that. She was there—at the end. My mom chose MAID, Medical Assistance in Dying, so she could die quietly at home at the time of her choosing. Adele and I took comfort in that. I miss her every day. She helped me raise Adele when I wasn't sure I could do it. I mean, twenty-two's not a teenager, but I was still completely unprepared. Hell, I didn't even know how to change a diaper. Mom taught me. Then she watched Adele while I found a job and tried to support all of us."

"Sounds rough."

He shook his head. "I'm glad...well, I shouldn't say I'm glad my sister died—because that would make me a horrible brother. Just... I thought when she had Adele that she'd straighten up. She didn't. So I'm glad Adele didn't have to grow up with a mother who chose drugs over and over again. I would've kept trying to get her clean, but she really wasn't interested."

"Jesus." I couldn't fathom.

"Yep. I miss my sister, but she was so sunk into her addiction that I'd spent little time with her in the years before she died. Mom?" His voice broke a little. "She's always been here."

Yet she'd never come to any of his performances. And when I'd hinted I wanted to meet her, he'd always had an excuse. I'd wondered if that was because I was Black, he was in the closet, or some combination.

That said, I never told him about the family farm. Had never brought him to Chilliwack.

He blinked, then shook his head. "Enough glumness. Tell me about yourself. How did you wind up selling goat's milk soap that smells divine?"

Yeah. Okay.

Chapter Five

Anderson

"One cherry and one Blue Moon shake." Sarabeth put them down with a flourish. Along with the straws. Paper—which really annoyed me. Then I'd remember I wanted to leave a better planet for Adele and I'd suck it up.

Jarrod gave her a dazzling smile. "This is awesome."

"Great. I'll be back with your food in a few minutes." Then she was gone.

The cherry shakes here were amazing, and the look of pure satisfaction on Jarrod's face assured me that he felt the same way. He sighed.

I sipped mine, enjoying the tang. "These are always the best."

"I'm glad you invited me." He rested his hand on the table.

I placed mine in his.

He squeezed. Then sighed. "Nothing much to say. I graduated and was working a great IT job with a major supermarket chain when my mom died. Suddenly, like. And I came home to help Dad with the funeral arrangements and never went back to my job. I've been working the farm for about twelve years now. Dad passed about five years back. He was all about selling the goat's milk. Never wanting to look beyond that." He rubbed his eyes with the hand I wasn't clutching. "When he died something...snapped. I hated farming. I really did. From time to time, I would take computer courses—refreshing my programming skills. I figured after Daddy died, I'd sell the farm and move back to the city."

"And yet you didn't."

"And yet I didn't." He offered a small smile. "The truth is, I love the goats. Most have passed, but I still have a couple of stubborn ones who've been around since I came home. Others have been born. I just—" He sighed. "I can't see myself just walking away and leaving them to someone else's keeping. I might hate farming, but I love my babies."

His eyes took on a glimmer. Whether he remembered goats who'd died—and wasn't that a weird thought—or remembrances of another kind, I couldn't be certain.

I took a deep breath, clinging to his hand. "Did you ever marry? Did you ever have kids?" Of the two of us, he'd been the one talking about adopting or surrogacy. I'd seen my name on a marquee somewhere.

Between the two of us, he'd had a much better shot at achieving his dream. Same-sex marriage had been legal in Canada for just over a year when we met. In the intervening years, a lot of barriers had dropped.

He shook his head. "I never came out to my dad. Didn't seem to be a reason to. If I'd met someone—" He eyed me. "If I'd met someone else... Well, I might've. But he was a traditionalist. Set in his ways. Why upset the proverbial applecart?"

"And after he died?"

A careless shrug. “Didn’t seem to be much point to looking. I had a good life. I was fulfilled in other ways. The farm’s paid for. Only problem is that I don’t have anyone to leave it to, you know? No one as a legacy. I suppose when I get closer to retirement, I’ll look at selling to someone keen. There’s a young woman at the neighboring farm. Her brother’s set to inherit the family’s cow farm. He’s a strong young man with a good head on his shoulders. But those two don’t always get along. I can’t see them working side-by-side with him being the owner. She’s planning to study agriculture at the university in the fall.”

I cocked my head. “The university in Abbotsford?”

He nodded.

“Well, that’ll be a shit ton less expensive than what Adele has planned. The University of Waterloo. Four-year undergrad degree in science and then the School of Optometry.”

He whistled. “That’s going to cost a fortune.”

“Yeah.” I scratched my stubbled chin. “I figure I’ll mortgage the house. It’s not like I have anything else to do with it.” *Or you can take Yvonne up on her generous offer and let her pay for Adele’s schooling.*

“Well, living without having to pay a mortgage might be nice.” He held my gaze. “You’re going to miss her, aren’t you?”

“She’s been my entire world for seventeen years.”

“No men?”

“I’ve got your food.” Sarabeth held out plates.

We both pushed our shakes to the side so she could put them down.

“Ketchup’s on the table. Don’t know why you’d want it, but there it is. You folks need anything else?”

“I think we’re good.” I offered her my best smile. “Thank you.”

“My pleasure.” She sashayed off. For someone so young—barely twenty-three—she had a great deal of confidence.

Jarrod cut a piece of his omelet. “I can’t wait.”

I eyed my burger. "Neither can I." Still, I started by popping a fry into my mouth. "Holy crap." I took a long drink of water. "How did I forget how hot these are?"

He grinned. "You always did prefer food on the tepid side." He put a large forkful of eggs into his mouth.

I rolled my eyes. "And you prefer fire-engine hot with both spice and temperature. Yeah, some things never change." I grabbed a knife to cut my burger in half. No way was I going to try to eat the monstrosity without cutting it down to size. "You know, Fifties makes the best burgers in Mission City."

He swallowed. "Best in Cedar Valley—but I still don't make it out this way too often."

"Yeah, that's fair."

"I could be persuaded to visit more often—if given the right inducement."

My cock perked up in interest. But I owed him honesty. "There've been a few guys over the years. Okay, like quite a few. Never at home, though. And Adele's never met any of them." *Because I never cared for any of them the way I cared for you.*

"Seventeen years is a long time to hide who you are."

I laughed. "Oh, Adele knows exactly who I am. She loves that her dad's gay. She keeps trying to set me up with any eligible guy who might even vaguely swing my way."

"And never succeeded?"

"Nope. She doesn't know I have a soft spot for leather daddies."

He held my gaze, his eyes wide.

I laughed. "That's what I told Shaw. Who told Damien. There are a few leather daddies around, but none have expressed any interest in me."

"I didn't know—"

My laughter continued. "I don't have a preference, if that's what you're thinking. I enjoy playing mind games with my boss and his husband. The truth is I've had all kinds of dates over the last fifteen or so years. Mostly one-night stands or one-month affairs. Never serious and, as I said, none ever met Adele."

"Ah." He took another bite of cheesy goodness.

I eyed my burger. "I've been lonely, Jarrod. Plain and simple. Every day I've regretted taking off and not telling you. I thought you might try to follow me. Give up your dreams to help me deal with my nightmare." Then I sighed. "No, Adele's not a nightmare. Burying my sister and cleaning up the mess she left behind was. For the first few years, I felt like I was barely holding things together. Mom worked, I worked, we shared child-rearing duties. When Adele started kindergarten, I felt like I could breathe for the first time. By then—" I sighed. "Seemed a little late to pick up the phone to apologize."

"Aside from the fact you would've found the number no longer in service?" He offered a smile. "I would've taken that phone call. Hell, I would've proudly introduced you to my parents. About the time you came up for air, my mama passed. So we were both at very different points in our lives."

"You always wanted kids." The words were out before I could check them.

"Yep. Never had any. And you didn't want to be tied down by them."

I winced. "Please don't ever repeat that to Adele. I've worked every single day to make sure she knows I have no regrets about leaving my old life behind to care for her. And I don't have any. Let's be honest—I wasn't *that* good of an actor. I wasn't going to be a god of the stage or the silver screen."

"Don't sell yourself short. You were damn talented."

"You were biased."

"You got great reviews, Anderson. You had the potential. Maybe a little refinement was needed, but you had a real shot. Then you vanished."

"I'll never be able to apologize enough for that."

"I accept your apology."

"Just like that?"

"Just like that. I could've resented my mama for dying or be angry at my daddy for coercing me to stay on the farm. Instead, I decided I was going to be mature and deal with the disappointments by being the best goat farmer around."

I blinked. "That's it?"

He grinned. "Yep. Although as soon as Daddy passed, I started making improvements. Started expanding."

"Hence the soaps."

"Yep. Been working on those for quite some time. Now I think I've got it perfected."

"I can't wait to try them."

"Well, you'll have to let me know what you think."

"Or you could come home with me and I'll show you." I bit into my burger.

His eyes went comically wide. "I thought you said—" He leaned in. "I thought you said you never brought guys home."

I swallowed. "They didn't mean anything to me."

"And I do?"

"You mean everything to me. Nothing's changed. I mean, I've grown up. And you're not the same boy I remembered."

He shook his head.

"But I still see we could do it, you know." I nabbed forkful of salad. "For old time's sake."

"Right..." A grin grew across his face. "For old time's sake. I like the sound of that."

"Maybe we could take our dessert to go?"

"We could take the rest of our meals to go." He nearly vibrated with excitement.

"Do you need to tend the goats?"

He shook his head. He pulled out his phone. "Mila will enjoy making a few extra dollars by taking care of them." He tapped. Then with a satisfied grin, he laid his phone on the table.

Without even time to pick up his fork, the thing buzzed.

He had true enthusiasm as he read the message. He met my gaze. "We're good."

"So let's eat. And then go home."

Chapter Six

Jarrod

Whatever I expected for Anderson's home, the charming house on Fifth Avenue wasn't it.

In fact, the thing looked more like a cottage with the yellow siding, sloped roof, and what I considered gingerbread accents. "It's lovely."

I'd followed him here and parked in the front as he indicated.

He parked around back and made his way to meet me at the front door.

"I grew up in this house. Come in."

Although we had yet to have snow, I had some mud on my boots, so I immediately removed them.

The space was compact. From the living room, I could see through to the dining room and then the kitchen.

"Let me take your coat, and then I'll give you the ten-cent tour."

He smiled as he helped me out of my red-and-black plaid jacket.

"You remind me of a lumberjack."

I gazed at his endearing face. He'd always been shorter than me. And our builds were so very different. He was lithe and nimble. I was stockier and more solid.

After he removed my coat, we stepped into the living room.

The couch had a vibrant red-rose floral design. The matching high-back arm chairs were a deep crimson that matched the pattern. The coffee table was a solid wood construction, and they faced a wood-burning fireplace.

Anderson waved. "I never use the thing. Bad for the environment. And I probably should've redecorated at some point. These were Mom's things, though. Adele's attached to them. I mean, we both miss my mom, but Adele clings to anything that denotes my mother's presence."

"Maybe when she goes away to university?"

He shrugged. "That's possible. But I'll be paying her tuition, residence, meals, books..." He winced.

I placed my arm against his shoulder blades. "You'll work things out."

"Yeah." He sighed. "Damien's sister-in-law, his dead wife's twin sister, has offered to pay for Adele's school."

"Really?" I found that hard to fathom. I didn't have any close friends—let alone ones who might consider helping me like that.

"Paget and Sedona's step-father, my boss, is..." He closed one eye—something he always did when he was deep in thought. "Well, wealthy would be the correct term, I suppose. The twins can go anywhere they want. Study anything they want. Apparently their aunt has been very careful with her savings and has the money to support Adele." He gestured. "My only other option is to mortgage the house. But I always saw this as Adele's future. Hell, I don't even know if she wants to come back to Mission City to be an optometrist."

"I'm sure someone here will be happy to have her join their practice. Or she can start her own." I kept my hand against his back—absorbing some of the warmth. He always had run hotter than me. In many ways.

"I didn't bring you back here to figure out my life's problems." He offered me a wicked smile.

Go with the flow. "Your bedroom, perchance?"

"Yep. There are two bedrooms and a small bathroom on the second floor. Adele and I were up there for years. When Mom died, my daughter encouraged me to move into the primary suite. I wouldn't have, but I realized she wanted more privacy. Sharing her bathroom with her dad was a bit much. I could've argued—" He shrugged. "—but she was a good kid who asked for very little. Granting her more space was the least I could do."

"Is it weird? Sleeping in your mom's room?"

"In that she died in the room? That brings a measure of comfort. She wanted to be with the people she loved in the house that meant so very much to her. I feel her spirit sometimes, you know? Like when I'm frustrated with Adele, I can hear Mom telling me to be patient." He turned to face me directly. "She would've loved you. I'm sorry I never gave you that opportunity."

"She lives through you. That's a precious gift."

His smile was a little shy. "She lives through Adele, too. She always told my daughter that she could do anything she set her mind to. Her mind is set on science, and I've nurtured that. She teased me today. Said she wanted to go to theater school. To follow in my footsteps."

I cocked my head. "Regrets?"

"No. Adele needed me. My mom needed me. I landed just fine—great job, great friends, great daughter..."

"But still lonely."

He bit his lower lip. "Well, yeah."

I pulled him close. "Not for tonight, okay?"

"Well, yeah."

He rested his head against my shoulder and I pulled him into my arms. So damn familiar—to the incongruous woodsy scent and his slim frame. Oh, and his ass that fit so perfectly in my hands. I whispered into his ear. "Make me remember."

A phrase we used all the time.

He pulled back to meet my gaze. "Yeah. That." Then he grinned. "But first I gotta put the dessert in the fridge." He pointed to the cloth bag he'd brought in and casually put on the coffee table.

"And I have to piss. Great milkshake. Better than I remembered."

"Yes, that. Why don't you use the guest bathroom upstairs? I hate to say this, but my daughter is more fastidious than I am."

I chuckled. "Yeah, okay." I'd spotted the staircase, so finding my way would be easy.

Just before I left him—even for just a few minutes—I drew him close.

He must've read my intentions, because he wrapped his arms around my neck and tugged me down for a kiss.

Where I thought I might get passion and fierceness—because that'd always been our specialty—I got tenderness. A quick brushing of the lips. A small taste of what was to come.

He pulled back, pecked my cheek, stepped away, grabbed the bag, then disappeared.

I headed up the stairs. As much as I wanted to shower, I figured we could do that afterward. So I did everything that needed to be done, then I headed back downstairs.

Anderson stood in the kitchen, trying to put the soaps, and other items he'd clearly bought at the market, up on a high shelf.

Instead of watching him struggle, I nabbed them and set them presumedly out of reach of teenage girls.

He laughed. "I love that you're taller than me and I'm jealous at the same time." He huffed. "Adele's taller than me as well."

"You're not worried she might find the gifts?"

"Uh, no. She does not spend her spare time in the kitchen."

"How will you get them down?"

"I guess you'll just have to be here to help me."

My heart beat faster.

"Or I can use the step stool."

My stomach sank.

He turned to place his hand on my chest. "I know which I'd prefer. Now, come to bed."

"With pleasure."

His bedroom was a soothing dove gray with burgundy accents—curtains, comforter, and throw pillows. "No floral?"

He laughed yet again. "Mom said I was free to redecorate. I let Adele help me—so that she didn't feel I was getting rid of her grandmother's things. They're in her hope chest—for when she feels ready to deal with them."

"Ah."

"My daughter—the sentimentalist." He grabbed the hem of his henley and yanked it over his head. "I doubt she got that from me."

Breathing proved difficult as he exposed all that perfect porcelain skin.

He arched an eyebrow. "I expect reciprocity."

"Yeah, okay." I'd worn a cable-knit sweater earlier, but the market proved warmer than I expected, so I'd stripped down to my T-shirt. Now, I untucked it from my jeans and yanked it over my head.

He just stared. "God, you're as beautiful as ever."

I didn't always feel beautiful. I wasn't slim like the other guys. I had a bit of padding around the waist. All that being said, I had decent muscles. The job required a lot of heavy lifting. "I don't know what to say."

"How about you strip and we get into bed and let our bodies do that talking? I know I've overshared tonight."

"No." I held his gaze. "There's no such thing. I want to know all about your life. I've missed so much of it." I wanted to demand that I not miss any more, but he likely wasn't in the right frame of mind to hear that. He needed time to adjust to the idea of having me in his life again. *If he lets me stay.*

Chapter Seven

Anderson

Something shifted in the room.

We'd alternated light and serious all night. What we hadn't done, in any great depth, was talk about the past.

I'd convinced myself—at the time and for the seventeen years after that—he'd been better off without me. That with a child, I would only weigh him down. Computer programmers weren't known for being sexy—stereotypes and all that—but I expected he'd found some high-paying job. That he was living the best life. Instead of at a farm a mere thirty miles away.

Is he happy? He says he could've sold when his dad died...

Really? This is what you're thinking about? You have a half-naked man in front of you.

I unbuttoned my jeans.

He licked his lips. Then mirrored my actions.

I was still as slender as the day I'd met him. Drove Damian nuts that I could eat just about anything and not gain a pound.

Oh well.

I yanked down jeans and underwear—carefully. I wasn't fully hard yet...but I was getting closer.

He pulled down his jeans. Then with a bit of a striptease, he lowered his boxers.

This time, I licked my lips.

His cock took notice.

"May I...?" I gestured.

"Oh God. I don't..." He palmed his cock. "I don't want to come too soon. I mean, if you still—"

"Like it up the ass? Oh hell, yes. I'm still vers, but I prefer bottoming."

He grinned. "Glad to see some things don't change."

I stepped toward him.

He met me halfway.

I twined my arms around his neck and dragged him down for a kiss. Not gentle, as it had been before. No, this kiss was tongues twining. This was a fight for dominance.

As usual, he won.

I always let him win.

His tongue swept through my mouth as he pressed his cock against mine. He reached between us and brought our cocks together. He tugged.

I broke away. "Do that and I'll come too soon. Refractory periods are a thing."

He chuckled. "Joys of getting old."

"Speak for yourself."

"I'm thirty-nine."

I scowled. "I hit forty a couple of weeks ago."

He chuckled. "I'll hit forty in January."

"I remember." January fifteenth. A day that never passed without me thinking of him. "Maybe...you'll let me take you out for dinner?" *Assuming we ever get around to having sex.* My arms were still twined around his neck as I gazed into his eyes.

"That's a month from now."

"I know."

"You're sure you'll still be in my life a month from now?"

I bit my lower lip—then nodded.

"Then I accept." He rubbed his cheek against mine. "You have condoms? I mean, I haven't—" He stopped.

I pulled back to meet his gaze. "I always have condoms. There's a box in Adele's bathroom as well. I don't want to think about my baby girl having sex—but I also don't want her to consider not being safe."

"You're a good dad."

"I try. I honestly do." I held his gaze. "What were you going to say?"

"That I haven't been with anyone."

For a moment, I couldn't figure out what he meant. I blinked. "Since college?"

He nodded.

"And I was your first."

He nodded.

"So..."

"My one and only."

That hit me like a fist to the solar plexus. Once Jarrod had figured out the mechanics of sex, he'd been game—anytime, anywhere. He loved sex. I couldn't fathom—

He pressed a kiss to my lips. "Don't overthink it."

"I can't believe..." Because I couldn't. Once I felt truly comfortable leaving Adele and Mom alone for the night, I started taking lovers. Well, hookups. Not a ton—but certainly more than none. "I'm sorry."

"Why? I'm not. I know how to join an app. Or a dating site. Or...whatever. Hell, I could've strolled Davie Street in downtown Vancouver." He held my gaze. "I think I'm, I dunno, demi? I like sex—but I've only ever wanted to have it with you."

Because you never met someone else. It sounds like you never even tried.

I nuzzled his neck. "You pull back the comforter, and I'll grab lube and condoms. I've never gone without a condom—except with you. I get tested regularly, but I'm due and I've been with a guy—" *Or two.* "—since the last time I was tested."

"Thank you." He pressed our lips together again.

As he grabbed the comforter, I opened my nightstand. Why I kept condoms there, I couldn't be certain. Like a responsible adult, I swapped them out after they expired.

Oh good. These haven't hit the expiration date yet. Woohoo!

I totally would've raided Adele's stash—but I appreciated not having to.

Jarrod lay on the middle of the bed, with a couple of pillows propped behind his head.

"Oh, like that, is it?" I waggled my eyebrows.

"Baby, I'll take you however I can get you. But I've dreamt of you riding my cock for the past seventeen years. How about you make my dreams come true?"

I swallowed the lump in my throat, shoving away the thought that I should've just come clean about Adele. Should've given him the choice. Should've at least have said goodbye—instead of leaving him hanging for all these years.

Instead of moping, though—and regretting the past—I hopped on my bed and made my way between his thighs.

"Do you want me to prep you?" He pointed to the lube.

I shook my head and tossed him the condom. "You do you and, this time, I'll do me. Maybe next time." My cock leaked a drop of precum. Suddenly I needed him inside me so badly that the idea robbed me of breath.

He grinned and ripped the condom packet open.

I sat back on my ass, spread my thighs, and started prepping myself. I didn't mind him doing this—when we weren't in a hurry. Adele might not be coming back for twelve hours, but I still felt like we needed to rush this.

"Oh baby, that is so fucking sexy." He uttered the words on a long exhalation.

I scissored and twisted and opened myself up as much as possible. I wasn't aiming for my prostate, though. I just wanted to get him inside me.

He held open his arms.

Since he'd lubed himself up, I allowed him to position me so I straddled his thighs.

Slowly, inch by inch, I sank onto him.

The burn was quick, intense, and passed just as fast.

I relaxed as he filled me. I placed my hands on his belly—that might've been a little softer than when we were younger. His arms and thighs, though, were solid muscle. He had the body of someone who worked physical labor for a living. I was as soft as they came—except I liked to swim while Adele played badminton. My nod to *exercise*.

Jarrod ran his hands up and down my thighs.

"I'm ready."

He grinned. He grasped my hips and guided me so I moved up and down on his cock.

The rhythm was achingly familiar. Seventeen years vanished in a heartbeat as his intense gaze met mine.

He ran his hands up my belly and tweaked my nipples.

My cock leaked.

He grinned. Yeah, he hadn't forgotten how to bring me to a frenzy in a short span of time. "I thought you wanted this to last."

"Oh, I hear refractory periods are a thing. We've got all night, baby. I intend for you to be sore in all the right places tomorrow."

My cock leaked more precum as I continued a steady rhythm. My prostate sang with each thrust, and I had to fight to keep my emotions in check. *Can't have you bawling while he's fucking you.*

Except this wasn't fucking. This was us—reconnecting. This was us finding a sense of belonging that had been missing in my life all these years. This was us searching for a way to make things work. We could still be together if we were no longer compatible sexually—but it sure helped we were on the same page.

He encircled my cock with his large hand. Experimentally, he gave it a tug.

I gasped. "Yeah, that works."

Again, he grinned.

I continued to ride him as he jerked me off.

"Don't want to come before you." I pushed the words out through gritted teeth.

"Please do. I need you to come, Anderson. More than you'll ever know."

I believed him. Even as he continued to work my cock, my balls drew up. "I'm coming."

He twisted his wrist—applying just the right amount of pressure to push me right over the edge.

Cum spurted out of me as my body flew high and light exploded behind my eyes. My vision narrowed as the orgasm overtook me entirely.

He grasped my hips and thrust upward with force. Then he held himself still as he stiffened. He closed his eyes and arched his neck as his body trembled.

When I started come down, I took stock. Cum everywhere? Yep. Totally blissed out? For certain. No longer able to keep myself upright? Yes to that as well. So I flopped onto his chest and he slipped from me. A feeling of emptiness overwhelmed me and, again, the tears threatened.

Then he wrapped his massive arms around me and I held me close. He whispered in my ear, "I never forgot you. And I never will."

Chapter Eight

Jarrod

I never forgot you. And I never will.

As I heated up some chocolate lava cake, those words came back to me.

I'd whispered them.

Anderson had cuddled against me.

And he'd promptly fallen asleep.

Sheesh.

Eventually, he'd rolled off and curled into a ball. Tempted as I was to spoon him and hold him forever, a couple of things couldn't wait—the condom and the sticky cum all over me.

Also all over Anderson, but that wasn't quite as critical.

I disposed of the condom in his bathroom and hopped into the shower. While managing to keep my hair dry, I also washed away the remnants of our mind-blowing lovemaking session.

My stomach had rumbled.

Remembering the nights of eating brownies after making love, back all those years ago, I decided to heat up the lava cake. I'd coax some into him and we'd either make love again, or he'd at least let me clean him up.

As the microwave beeped, I heard a noise.

When the final beep sounded, a young woman appeared in the doorway of the kitchen.

Yeah, no doubt who this is.

That was my first thought. The second, and far more important, was to thank Christ I'd put on my boxers and jeans. Even though they weren't done up.

All the blinds were closed against the dark near-winter night...so I'd considered not putting anything on.

"I'm Adele." Boldly, she held out her hand.

I took her hand. Her grip impressed me as we shook. "Jarrod."

Finally, she let me go. "I figured. Uncle Damien said something about Dad meeting up with an old friend. Since he has never, to my knowledge, brought someone home, I didn't think anything of coming home."

"It's almost midnight." A glance at the microwave clock told me that.

"Paget started throwing up. At first Uncle Shaw thought she just ate too much popcorn—which wouldn't be like her, but we all get upset stomachs from time to time."

"Uh-huh."

"Uncle Damian took her temperature, and it's super high. I decided I'd rather come home than risk catching something." She pointed to the microwave. "That said, we sat next to each other at the cinema, were all in my car, and then we crashed in the media room at their house. I'd say if she's sick, I probably have it too. Still, I just wanted to come home."

"And they just let you leave?"

She waved me off. "I sent a DM to the family chain when I got home. Uncle Shaw responded that Paget's still sick and to take care." She eyed me. "I'm seventeen."

"I'm aware." I opened the microwave and gingerly pulled the plate out. I put it on the kitchen table.

"Oh my God. Is that lava cake from Fifties?" She might've squealed that.

"You're welcome to have some. Is your stomach okay?" I didn't want to feed her something that might make her ill later.

She waved me off again. "I'm fine. Rock-solid stomach. Paget's always been a bit sensitive. I'm more like Sedona—a rock."

"These are Shaw and Damien's twins?" I opened the first cupboard and found glasses. I pulled three down. "Water? Milk?"

"Yeah, they're the twins." She cocked her head. "So how much of an *old friend* are you to my dad. I'll get the milk." She headed to the fridge.

I blinked. "We...well...college." I cleared my throat.

"So before I was born."

"Yeah."

"Uh-huh. You know, he never talks about that. Grandma used to tell me about his talent acting."

"She never came to see his shows."

Her gaze shot to mine. "She worried she'd make him too nervous. I think, later on, she regretted that. Especially when she couldn't convince him to try amateur theater out here."

"Your father is incredibly talented."

She poured a glass of milk. Then held the jug as if to ask me.

I nodded.

"You know he's really my uncle, right?"

"He considers you his child. Never doubt that." I could say this with absolute certainty. I knew Anderson. Had always known him. Hopefully still did.

"I know." She opened another cupboard and grabbed three plates. "I assume Dad's joining us? Or were you sneaking around?"

I laughed. "I was going to take him some in bed. Seemed the considerate thing to do."

She waved me. "Don't let me interfere. I'll take my third and head upstairs with my milk." She pursed her lips. "Are you going to be here in the morning?"

"I hadn't thought that far." Well, I had—but I didn't want to be presumptuous. Mila was taking care of my goats—I could afford to stay overnight.

"I can make myself scarce in the morning."

"You don't have to do that." Anderson wandered into the kitchen, wearing a bathrobe. He gave me a glance that was a cross between panic and relief.

Probably panic that Adele was home and relief I wasn't totally naked.

He pulled her into an embrace. "Everything okay?"

"Yeah. Paget's sick."

His gaze sharpened. "And you?"

"I'm fine, Dad. I wouldn't have driven home if I wasn't feeling fine."

Still, he pressed a hand to her forehead.

I suppressed the longing. Such a simple gesture—parent to child. Witnessing it sort of stole my breath.

She swatted his hand away.

This close, I was able to see she actually had several inches on him. Since he wasn't all that short, she was quite tall.

"Let's eat the cake before it cools and I have to heat it up again." Because standing here talking with me in just my jeans, with my smattering of chest hair, wasn't weird at all.

Anderson's eyes lit. "Yes, please."

Adele sat on a chair with a leg tucked under her.

Her father opened the cutlery drawer. He handed me a knife and put three forks on the table.

Our gazes met.

I read gentle compassion. Mixed with a bit of gratitude. I sat and proceeded to cut the cake into three equal pieces. The cake wasn't actually that large and split three ways made it even less—but it would satisfy my craving for chocolate. Something that often happened after sex.

Which I was quite certain Anderson remembered.

Adele sank her fork into the concoction—crispy on the outside with gooey warm melted chocolate in the middle. "Okay, so Uncle Damien said you were 'old friends'." She used air quotes.

Again, my gaze sought Anderson. His daughter appeared pretty sharp—she'd figured out what we'd been doing. I'd answered her question earlier—but evasively. Clearly she wasn't going to let that rest.

"We were lovers." Anderson pressed his knee against mine under the table. "And I hurt him."

"You didn't—"

He glared.

I sighed. "Yeah, okay, you did."

"And I'm sorry for that."

"Is this because he came home to take care of me? Was I the cause of the heartache?"

"No." Anderson and I said the word at the same time.

She rolled her eyes.

"No," Anderson reiterated. "I was happy to make the choice. Don't ever doubt that. Things might've been...unorthodox. And I miss your mother a lot—"

"She was a drug addict." Adele took a bite of cake.

Anderson jerked, as if struck. "I never—"

"Grandma told me. Just before she died. She wanted to make certain I understood what you'd done. What you'd sacrificed. She also wanted to warn me that drugs were never the way out. I think, because she saw me as sensitive, that I might fall into that trap."

"Trap?" I asked the question since Anderson was still a little pale.

"Drugs. Drinking. Random sex with strangers."

"Ah." This time, Anderson spoke. "She never told me."

"She didn't want you to worry. You had enough going on without dealing with any crap that might come my way as a teenager and then as an adult." She forked another piece. "I wasn't into that stuff anyway."

"You might when you go to university. When you're away from home for the first time." A bit of color had returned to his cheeks.

That reassured me.

Somewhat.

"Aunt Yvonne's money." She scrutinized her fork. "I'm going to study my ass off. I want to get into the optometry school—that's one of the toughest programs in the country."

"That's ambitious." I grinned. "I like your spirit."

"And before you fret, Dad, I have a backup plan."

"Teaching or medical school." His even tone didn't fool me. This was overwhelming him.

"Well, you'll have Jarrod to keep you company. I'm off to bed. I'll be careful in the morning." She hopped up. She moved to her dad and pressed a kiss to his temple. "I like him." She winked at me. Then she popped the last piece of cake in her mouth. As she chewed, she rinsed her plate and put it into the dishwasher. Then she downed the last dregs of her milk, then put the glass in the dishwasher as well. She gave a little wave and then clomped up the stairs.

I cleared my throat.

Anderson's gaze shot to mine.

"I like her."

He cracked a smile. "I think she liked you too."

I placed my hand on his as it rested by his plate. "I have no expectations—"

His eyes narrowed. "Do you want this to mean something? I know it's really soon...but I never forgot you. Never stopped wondering how you were doing. Holding myself back from calling you was hard. But I'd hurt you—or at least I thought I had. And staying away from you was the price to pay for that hurt."

"No. I never saw it like that. I always assumed you had a reason for what you did. And, for the record, I could've searched you out. I could've made the effort. But I valued you—and your decision."

"I was wrong." He blinked. "Really wrong."

"You did what you had to do with the cards you were dealt—I respect that. I always have and I always will. Don't feel sorry for me. I've made a good life for myself. In my own way, I'm happy. Now...would I be happier with you in my life? Possibly." I squeezed his hand. "Probably."

He cleared his throat. "Where do we go from here?"

"We finish our cake and milk, and then we go back to bed. We have your daughter's permission, after all." I grinned.

After a long moment, he smiled back. "Yeah, that sounds good."

And so we did.

Chapter Nine

Anderson

I awoke with a strong arm banded around my chest and a very interested cock poking me in the ass.

Jarrod pressed a kiss to my shoulder. "You're awake?"

"Yep." I pressed his hand to my sternum. "Have you heard the elephant clomp down the stairs?"

He chuckled. "No, I haven't heard anything resembling either an elephant or a teenage girl."

I wiggled my butt.

His hand meandered down my side and grasped my hip. He pulled me back against him and thrust his cock against my ass. He hummed in what I interpreted to be satisfaction.

"Roll onto your back."

He paused in his nuzzling of my neck.

"I want to give you a blow job—so roll onto your back."

"Okay." He sounded skeptical, and I was pretty certain I knew the reason. He was all about giving pleasure—but rarely sank into the bliss himself until his partner had orgasmed. Or had come damn close.

Still, he settled back into the middle of the bed and put his hands behind his head—interlacing his fingers. His eyes were still a little droopy as he slowly pulled himself from slumber. He was a little sluggish in the morning waking up. Coffee was a necessity for him. I couldn't imagine getting up early with farm animals. "Hey, how early do goats get up?"

He laughed. "Don't worry about my goats. Mila will call if there's a problem."

That hadn't been my concern, but his beautiful cock curving up toward his belly—with a drop of precum leaking—captured my attention. I eased his thighs apart so I could settle in between them.

He grinned.

I licked the tip of his cock, savoring the tang of his precum on my tongue.

He moaned.

Slowly, I pulled him into my mouth. I swirled my tongue around his crown as I sucked. Still, I held his gaze.

He grasped my hair in those large hands—whether to hold me in place or to encourage me, I couldn't be certain. The one thing I did know for sure was that he loved it when I sucked him off.

I tongued his slit.

He nearly bucked off the bed.

I swallowed him deeper.

He thickened in my mouth.

I grasped his balls and rolled them around in my hands.

Another moan. His eyes drifted shut as I hollowed my cheeks and sucked for all I was worth. He tried to tighten his thighs, but I held them apart with my shoulders. With my other hand, I circled his rim.

"I'm coming, Baby. Please—"

That was as far into his warning as he got. He stiffened, then shot cum into my mouth. I swallowed as much as I could, but there was just too much, and a bit dribbled out of the corner of my mouth.

Still, I kept sucking—wanting every last drop of him.

He shuddered. His grip on my hair loosened, and he stroked my cheek gently. "Oh Baby."

I grinned. Then I crawled up his body and gave him a kiss. A toe-curling, tongues-clashing, deep-drugging kiss.

He grasped my cheeks and encouraged me to come even closer. To meld our bodies together. "You haven't come." He whispered the words.

"I'm good." I chuckled. "I just wanted to see you climax."

"I want to return the favor."

Yet I didn't want him to. As much as a blow job would've been nice, I wanted him to continue to sink—and revel into—his bliss.

"You really want me to come?"

He nodded. "Please. That."

I scooted back, so I straddled his hips. Mindful of his very deflated cock, I positioned myself. Then I took myself in hand. Just six tugs and my balls drew up. I came all over him. *More showers and washing sheets.* I grinned even as I sank into the fantastic orgasm.

"Come here." He held out his arms.

I eyed my spunk all over his chest. *We're going to shower anyway.*

We did...eventually.

And since I was hornier than at any point in the last seventeen years, we also exchanged hand jobs in the shower.

After we dressed, stripped the bed, and put on fresh sheets, we made our way to the kitchen—following our noses and, more particularly, the smell of sizzling bacon.

Adele greeted us with a shit-eating grin on her face. "I was going to suggest Fifties, but then I decided a nice brunch at home was in order. I've cooked up pancakes, French toast, and eggs are just waiting for their marching orders."

Jarrod chuckled. "French toast is more than enough for me. My favorite."

"And bacon." She eyed him—as if daring him to give the wrong answer.

"Yes, please." He grinned.

She nodded. For all of her environmental activism—and I'd gotten plenty of lectures about my profligate lifestyle—she couldn't bring herself to give up bacon or hamburgers. Even though *cow farts are ruining the atmosphere.*

"Is there anything we can do?" Jarrod glanced around the kitchen and, undoubtedly, saw what I saw. Table set. Kitchen counters mostly free of pots, pans, or anything else. Adele always managed to clean as she went, but even after forty years on this planet, I hadn't managed to figure that one out.

She pointed to the table. "Let me grab the plate out of the oven."

Moments after we'd plopped our butts, she procured a plate piled high with thick-cut golden-colored French toast and pancakes clearly cooked to perfection.

My throat felt a little raw as I swallowed. "Thanks, sweetie."

She arched an eyebrow as she put the plate on a coaster.

"Sorry. Thank you, Adele." Because we'd had that conversation. Just because I wanted her to stay little forever, didn't mean she was willing to. Sixteen had been her hard limit. I could call her *daughter* or *Adele*. That was all she'd tolerate.

Jarrod stifled a laugh.

"Oh yeah, you try turning off something you've done for, I dunno, their entire lives."

A stillness overtook him.

Shit. "I'm sorry—that was insensitive of me."

Adele plated the bacon on top of a couple of paper towels. She pressed another on top to soak up some of the grease. "For Dad's cholesterol." She put the plate on the table.

Jarrod eyed me.

"She's joking. I had a physical a couple of months ago, and all's good. Should I be paying closer attention to my diet? Probably." I lifted the paper towel and offered the plate to him.

He held my gaze as he took two slices.

"You can have more than that." Adele slid into her chair. "I pulled a few pieces when they were nice and cooked and let the rest burn to a crisp."

"My favorite." Still, I held Jarrod's gaze.

"Glad to see some things don't change." He turned to Adele. "I'm mighty grateful. I prefer less blackened."

"I thought you might. Not everyone loves charbroiled."

"Hey." I tried faux indignation. "You prefer it that way as well."

"There's no accounting for taste." She rolled her eyes.

Jarrod smiled. "Well, then I doubly thank you for cooking them the way I like."

Adele's gaze softened. "I want you to be happy." She eyed me. "Because you seem to make Dad happy. He was all stressed yesterday."

I glared. "Not stressed—"

"You thought you'd have to pay for eight years of university—including a professional program."

I winced.

She waved me off—as she often did. "Aunt Yvonne wants to come over tomorrow night so we can talk specifics. Her expectations of me, what she will and won't pay for...all that stuff."

Jarrod pressed his knee against mine.

"That would be lovely." I offered a smile. Best I could do as I thought about someone else paying for my baby girl's education.

"Plus, I've applied for a ton of scholarships and bursaries. Anything I might qualify for. And I'm working all summer at the pool. Oh..." Her eyes lit. "And if I get accepted into the co-op program at Waterloo, then I have a work semester between my school terms. It takes an extra year, but I'll have work experience and extra money."

I tried to absorb all that. "Is that program tougher to get into?"

"Yep." She grinned. "Which means I just have to study harder. Are you going to be around this afternoon? I want to spread out on the dining room table."

"I don't see how whether or not I'm here affects your studying."

"Caleb wants to come over, and it'll be crowded if you and, uh—"

"Jarrod. You can call me Jarrod."

She grinned. "If you and Jarrod are here."

I wanted to make a comment about having a boy over while I wasn't here. In confidence, though, she'd let me know Caleb was gay. Just not out because of his religious conservative family. He was always a respectful young man, so I certainly couldn't argue on those grounds.

"I was going to invite your father to see my farm."

My gaze shot to Jarrod.

He gave me the *just go with it* look I always found endearing. He could always tell when I was in over my head—and he'd offer me a lifeline.

"I'd love to see the farm." Because I honestly did. I wanted to know everything about the life Jarrod had built for himself.

"That's great." He beamed.

Takes so little to make him happy.

Had I ever been that way? It felt like such a very long time ago.

"Great." Adele leapt up. "I'm going to put the dishes in the dishwasher, have a shower, and then get cracking on the books."

"Right." I met Jarrod's gaze. "I guess my day is free."

"I can't wait for you to meet the goats."

Adele stilled. "Goats? Like those cute little things who do goat yoga?"

Jarrod blinked. "Uh, my goats don't do yoga. They produce goat milk."

"Oh. That's too bad. Goat yoga sounds like fun." She stacked the dishes and took them over to the dishwasher.

I was sort of surprised to see we'd demolished the pile of French toast as well as all the bacon. I eyed the pancakes. "Can you save them for later?"

"Of course." She came over with a container and handed it to me. Then she went back to the dishwasher. "They're Caleb's favorite—so I might've been grateful you didn't eat them all."

Jarrod rubbed his belly. "Those were mighty fine French toast slices. Better than anything I might've cooked up."

"You're welcome to come over whenever." Adele shut the dishwasher and turned it on. "Dad insisted I learn how to cook. I do a mean eggplant parmesan."

I nodded my agreement. "Far superior to anything I might throw together."

Adele pecked my cheek. "That's because Uncle Shaw keeps you busy at work."

A familiar refrain. I'd told her about a million times that I enjoyed working long hours to keep Shaw organized. I also made it clear she'd always be my priority. Keeping that balance had been easier with Mom around. Now I was truly a single parent. "I can't believe you turned out to be such a great kid."

She rolled her eyes. "You always say that."

"Maybe because it's always true. When's your next shift at the pool?"

"I'm teaching lessons on Tuesday night." She gave Jarrod a brilliant smile. "I'm a lifeguard. Have been for a year now. I do love teaching."

"Yet you want to be an optometrist."

"Yep." She gave a little shrug. "Perhaps a little incongruous, but it is what it is." She did a little pirouette and pranced out of the room.

I laughed. "All those dance lessons and, in the end, she enjoys recreational badminton and swimming more. I thought she might do it competitively, the swimming, but she really loves working with kids."

"Kids need glasses too." He shrugged.

"That's true—she'll be amazing with them." I placed my hand on the table.

He grasped it. "Farm?"

"Yeah. Sounds great. I'll have to drive, though, because I'm not asking you to make a round trip."

"I wouldn't mind."

"Maybe. But you've got goats who've missed you."

He grinned. "Oh, Mila will have taken good care of them. Even spoiled them a bit."

"If you say so." I squeezed his hand. Then I let go and pushed away from the table.

We stood at the same time.

He held open his arms.

I stepped into them.

He squeezed me. "They always grow up too fast."

"Goats?"

"Uh, no. I meant kids." He chuckled. "Although baby goats are called kids..."

On that, we both laughed.

I rubbed my cheek against his stubbled jaw. "I've missed you."

He sighed, pressing a kiss to my cheek. "Not as much as I've missed you. Let's go."

And so we did.

Chapter Ten

Jarrod

I shouldn't have been nervous bringing Anderson home with me—and yet I was. I drove carefully, always keeping sight of him in my rearview mirror. I'd provided him with my address—in case we got separated—but he kept pace with me and pulled into the driveway behind me.

Mila stepped out from the clapboard-sided white two-story farmhouse. I tried to ignore the peeling paint and the sagging porch step. Always on my to-do list...but never quite getting done.

"Hey, Jarrod." She waved. "They missed you."

I exited my truck, locked it, and stepped toward her.

Anderson was just behind me.

"I appreciate you taking care of them for me." I gestured. "This is my friend, Anderson." I caught his gaze. "This is the woman who keeps me sane. Mila."

She stepped forward with her arm outstretched.

Anderson took it.

I caught his eyes widening slightly.

Yep, Mila had a hell of a grip—and wasn't afraid to use it. Anything to prove she was as competent as her brother.

"I was just going to give Anderson a tour."

"Cool. I need to be getting home. Give me a call if you need me. Otherwise, I'll be here Tuesday morning." She worked for me Tuesday, Thursday, and Sunday mornings. Theoretically so I could sleep in—but I never did. I appreciated her help, though. "Oh, how did the market go?"

"Sold out. That's why I'm not there today. I wasn't the only one, either. I feel kind of bad for the people who turn up today, but I found a guy who knits sweaters to take my table. They look so damn comfortable, I considered buying one for myself."

"Hopefully he gets good sales. Nice to meet you, Anderson." She waved and then headed over to her pickup truck. Moments later, she was gone.

"She's—" Anderson squinted.

"Yeah. Five feet of pure determination and muscle and drive."

"Adele would tower over her."

"Adele towers over you." I nudged him.

He rolled his eyes. "My sister once said Adele's father was tall. That was pretty much the only time she spoke of the guy."

"Has he ever come around?"

"No." He toed a piece of gravel—thereby not looking me in the eye. "I have worried about that. I loved my sister, but she rarely hung out with anyone who might qualify as a *good* crowd. I don't even know if the guy was aware she was pregnant. She didn't list anyone on the birth certificate."

I gestured for us to wander toward the house.

He fell into step beside me.

"Do you worry?"

"We had a long conversation about DNA databases. That she might find out things she doesn't want to know."

"Yikes. Something I'd never even considered." I held open the screen door and gestured for him to go in the bright-red-painted front door.

He did, then immediately removed his shoes.

I laughed as I closed the door. "All the flooring is vinyl. Replaced two years ago. I'd go nuts if I always had to take off my boots—unless they're covered in mud. I just sweep up regularly."

"That's fair. I'll still remove mine." He offered me a shy smile. His eyes shone in the sunlight pouring in through the window near the top of the door.

"You want a tour?"

"Absolutely." He clapped his hands and grinned in what I could only interpret as giddiness.

"It's not all that exciting."

He pressed his index finger to my lips. "This is *your* home—of course it's exciting."

"Well, okay, then. Why don't we start upstairs? Then we can do the downstairs and end up in the barn where you can meet the goats?"

"I was kind of hoping to end the tour with your bedroom." Said with just the right amount of lasciviousness.

"So you're not worried about getting home?"

He waved off my concern. "Adele's a good kid. Caleb's a sweetheart. I'd be holed up in my room working anyway."

I arched an eyebrow.

"Oh, my old bedroom. Upstairs. I converted it into a den. Sloped ceilings, a dormer window, and a view over all of Cedar Valley. I'm often distracted by the scenery." He gestured to the mountains to the north of me, across the Fraser River. "You've got a pretty stunning view."

"Yeah." I grinned. "Okay, goats first."

He put his boots back on and, since neither of us had removed our coats, we headed back outside.

The ground was pretty solid under our feet. We'd had snow earlier in the autumn, and a bit again last week, but it'd melted. "You, uh, think we're going to have a white Christmas?" I opened the gate and let him through. After securing it, I kept walking.

He fell into step beside me. "We've had quite a few over the past few years. More than I remember in my childhood. I thought the climate was warming."

"Stand aside." I gestured for him to stand behind me. I opened the door to the barn and a few bleats sounded before a little horde of goats came out into the yard.

Sassy came straight toward me, finding me as if I had a homing beacon. She bleated her displeasure with me.

"I was only gone a day." I rubbed her ears.

Joseph examined Anderson with such intensity that even I wondered what the cantankerous guy was thinking.

"Joseph, this is Anderson."

Anderson waved.

My goat blinked.

"Is he going to hurt me?"

I considered. "Probably not, but don't ever leave your shoes lying around."

Anderson gave me a skeptical look. "Why would I take my shoes off while within reach of a goat?"

I was about to tell him about the time— Nope. No point. "I'm just warning you."

"Okay." He waved to Joseph. "Nice to meet you."

My goat continued to stare.

"This is Sassy. She's—" I continued rubbing her ears.

"A suck?"

"Well, she is that. She loves attention. Can never get enough of it."

"May I pet her?"

"Of course. She'd love it. I'm just going to check on the others." I left him to it as I checked the barn for any stragglers. "Come on, Lucinda. You can't hide. You need to go out into the pasture while the weather's still good."

Stubborn goat stood facing the wall. If she couldn't see me, her reasoning was, then I couldn't see her.

This was a game we frequently played.

I made my way over to her.

She gazed up at me.

"I might have a treat for you."

Reluctantly, she followed.

I scooped some oats into my palm when we passed the feeder.

She happily took some from my palm. When we emerged into the brilliant sunlight, she headed over to the pasture with the others.

Anderson was still scratching Sassy's ears.

"I warn you—she'll never tire of that."

He grinned. "I think I don't mind. They're—" He gazed over the field. "Precious."

"Yeah. You can see how, after I came home, I couldn't consider leaving them."

"Even to Mila?"

I shook my head. "But I'm considering bringing her on as a partner. I want to expand. That's not just expensive, but it would be a huge commitment."

"Do you think she'd agree to it?"

"You know, I think she would. She's tired of her brother always bossing her around. Hell, I don't mind when she gives me a piece of her mind. She's made a few great suggestions."

"Like goat yoga?" Anderson gazed into Sassy's dark-brown eyes. "You would just love to step on people while they stretched, wouldn't you?"

Damn goat bleated her agreement.

"Seriously?" I scratched my chin. "I can't really imagine it."

"Well, you could offer the yoga classes. Do you invite kids from local schools to visit?"

"Uh...no."

"You might consider that. Although liability's always an issue."

I rolled my eyes. "I've got tons of insurance. Takes up a damn lot of my expenses—but I try to be prepared for anything."

"What about having families visit? You remember the figurines?"

I blinked. "Oh, yeah. Henry makes them."

"Right. He's married to Johnson—who runs a cider-making business. He also gives tours of the orchard and has picking parties in the fall."

"Well, I reckon that makes sense."

"Wyatt and Tate run a pumpkin patch. Again, they have people visit them...like a destination."

"You're suggesting...?" I scratched my cheek. "That I invite strangers onto the property?"

"When you put it like that, it doesn't sound nearly as exciting. I'm saying what if you open the farm to families a couple of days a week? Give them the real *farm* experience. Kids are so tied to their electronics. I think it might be fun to play with goats. I know Adele would've loved it. I took her to a petting zoo once. One of her favorite memories."

I considered. "You really think so?"

He met my gaze. "Yeah, I really think you could. But, hell, this is your farm. You know what you can and can't do."

"Mila mentioned the goat yoga. I plum forgot about that. I'd have to pass the rest by her. Having guests is a lot of responsibility."

"You wouldn't have to go to markets—you could sell your soap here. Even show people how you make it. Unless that's giving up trade secrets."

"Anyone can find recipes on the internet."

"True." He looked up, as if taking in the pasture for the first time. "You'd need a website. I can take care of that. I can help you put together a marketing plan. Maybe have a grand opening in the spring?"

His eagerness couldn't be overstated—clearly this was something he really thought was a good idea.

"I should, like, have a business plan or something. Right?"

"Oh, I can help with that. My title might be *executive assistant*, but I've actually picked up quite a few things while working with Shaw. This would be—" He met my gaze.

My breath caught.

"I'm getting ahead of myself. This is your farm—you know what's best."

"But you've got great ideas. Clearly you're seeing something I've never considered. That doesn't mean they're not good ideas. It just means I might need some convincing."

He grinned. "I would be happy to do that."

"Let's get them fed so I can give you a tour."

"Ending up in your bedroom?"

"Yeah, that sounds good." I grasped his hand. "Why is it that I look at you and see my future?"

He swallowed. "I'm sorry."

"You don't need to be. You did what you had to do. I don't begrudge you that."

"You should."

I shook my head. "That's in the past. Like I said—when I look at you now, I see my future."

"Yeah. So do I."

We fed the goats. We washed our hands, had ham sandwiches, and I gave him a tour of the house—culminating in the bedroom.

After a rather torrid bout of lovemaking, we cuddled.

And strategized our future.

Epilogue

Anderson

"I can't believe I survived my first semester!" Adele sat on the sofa in the farmhouse and stretched her arms wide.

Yvonne chuckled. "You did. Great grades too." She had a self-satisfied smile on her face that reassured me she had no problems paying for my daughter's education.

Russell, our Australian shepherd, leapt into Adele's lap. She laughed as he licked her face.

"I can't believe you managed to rescue a dog who knows how to herd goats." She laughed.

The damn dog preened.

"He's a character." Jarrod wrapped an arm around my shoulder. "He's great with the visitors as well. Between herding them and keeping the goats in their proper place, he does well for himself. And rescue is relative."

Adele eyed him. "He needed a new home."

"Well, yes. The young couple who bought him didn't realize how much exercise he would need." Jarrod grinned. "Our luck we went looking for a rescue about the time they placed an ad for the guy."

As if knowing we were talking about him, Russell woofed.

Which got Rufus, Shaw's dog, woofing as well.

"Oh shush." Shaw glared at his dog.

Damien laughed—whether at his husband's antics or the dog's, I couldn't be certain.

"Your replacement isn't as competent as you." Shaw eyed me.

"I gave her plenty of training."

"He misses you." Paget poked Shaw.

"I miss him too."

"But not enough to be coaxed off the farm?" He pretended to be affronted. "I offered you a substantial raise."

"I happen to love the farm." I'd rented my house in Mission City to Caleb and his friend Roxanne—another queer kid rejected by her family. They were taking good care of the house as they worked hard and saved to do college classes at night.

Shaw, of course, upon learning of their situation, had offered to pay for their schooling.

I hadn't felt comfortable making the offer. So, Adele was going to do it after Christmas.

Sedona sat on the floor and cuddled Rufus. "I think it's so cool this is your first Christmas as a married couple." She was very much into pairing everyone up these days.

Damian had warned Yvonne. Just in case she didn't want her niece matchmaking.

At the Christmas market, I'd caught Yvonne gazing at a striking woman in a purple coat and with a blonde pixie cut and wide green eyes.

I hoped, if she was single, that she might be interested in my friend.

"Old married couple." Jarrod snickered. "Just took us twenty years to get here."

Shaw grinned. "I can't believe you never told me about your first love."

"Some secrets are meant for a man to keep to himself." I pressed a kiss to Jarrod's cheek.

He turned to face me. After holding my gaze for a moment, he nodded.

"And some secrets are made to share." I grinned.

Adele sat up straight, and poor Russell got tossed to the floor.

He yelped—more from surprise than any injury—and promptly leapt onto Sedona's lap.

She cooed and cuddled him.

He licked her face as well.

I made a note to remind everyone to wash their hands before we sat down to Christmas dinner.

"Well, don't make us wait." Adele stomped her foot.

Jarrod chuckled.

I swallowed the lump in my throat. Her life was about to change forever—again. First, I started dating Jarrod seriously.

She insisted we make it official.

I pointed out Jarrod couldn't leave the farm, and she still needed me.

She'd huffed. Then pronounced she was moving in with Shaw and Damien so I could move to the farm.

That had stunned me—not only because she thought I'd let her—but also because I hadn't considered it. Not until that moment. Yes, I'd been working with Jarrod on plans for family-visiting days and goat yoga—because that really was a thing—but I hadn't thought about leaving Shaw. About leaving Mission City. Yes, Chilliwack was half an hour away, but—

Yvonne was the one who convinced me. She pointed out Adele would be leaving for university soon and needed to have more freedom. Damien and Shaw would take care of her while she could be more independent.

So, in May, Jarrod and I married. I moved in, and we set about creating a life together.

In September, Adele went to the University of Waterloo.

And in October— I blinked. "Okay. So, we found a surrogate over the summer."

Adele clenched her hands into fists as she continued to vibrate with anticipation. We'd broached this with her before the wedding, and she'd thrown her wholehearted support behind us becoming parents—however that might happen.

We'd begun to explore adoption when we came across Marisa. She was thrilled to be a surrogate for us. She was Black, like Jarrod, and so we'd opted to use his sperm. And it took.

"She's just past the twelve-week mark. Now, things can still go wrong." This was her third pregnancy. But the first with these particular circumstances.

"And?" Still, my daughter was clearly impatient, but clearly trying to rein herself in.

"Twins. We don't know the gender—" I didn't get any further as Adele launched herself at Jarrod.

I wasn't the least bit offended. This was going to be his first shot at parenthood—a dream come true for him.

And, honestly, for myself as well. Somehow diapers and late-night feedings and all that other stuff sounded great. We'd raise the twins on the farm—with a loving older sister, the adoring twin cousins, and the uncles we planned to ask to be godparents. Thus far, Shaw had avoided infants. I fully intended to teach him how to diaper a baby.

He pulled me into a hug. "I've never seen you so happy."

I met his gaze, blinking back the moisture. "I don't know what that says."

"That you're where you're meant to be. It's all good. I'll figure out the rest."

"I'm just a phone call away."

He rolled his eyes. "I know." He'd used that lifeline and called me about a dozen times over the last seven months. Some habits died hard, and I was always willing to help.

"I want cider." Yvonne rose. "I'll heat some." She headed to the kitchen.

"I'll help." Sedona followed her.

Adele pulled me into a big hug. "I'm so freaking happy for you."

"Yeah?" I met her gaze. "Really?"

"Didn't I say as much?"

"Yes. But saying you're okay with me having a baby—well, two babies—and the reality are two very different things."

She waved me off. "All good. Truly. I'm excited. Not many nineteen-year-olds will have baby brothers or sisters." She squinted. "You really don't know?"

I shook my head.

"You'd better call me first."

"Count on it." Jarrod wrapped his arm around her shoulders. "This is very much a family thing."

"Cool. I want hot chocolate." She grabbed Paget's hand. "We'd better get in there."

Given the size of the kitchen, we'd all fit easily.

Damien grabbed Shaw's hand. "We'll give you guys a minute." He whistled.

Rufus and Russell happily followed the couple into the kitchen.

"He's going to give them carrots." Both dogs were obedient pups when it came to their carrots. Jarrod smiled.

I laughed. "I can think of worse things to feed them."

He pulled me into his side.

I fit perfectly.

"You ready for this?"

My eyes widened. "Hell, fucking, no."

"Yeah, that's what I thought. I love you." He kissed my nose.

I hugged him tightly. "Best second chance ever."

"For keeps this time."

And so it was.

Want more Gabbi Grey?

Check out her Love in Mission City series, set in beautiful British Columbia.

The first book is

Ginger Snapping All the Way (Love in Mission City Book 1)

Also available:

Stanley's Christmas Redemption (Love in Mission City Book 2)

The Beauty of the Beast (Love in Mission City Book 2.5)

Sleigh Bells and Second Chances (Love in Mission City Book 3)
A Daddy for Christmas 2: Foster (Love in Mission City Book 3.5)
Rayne's Return (Love in Mission City Book 4)
Gideon's Gratitude (Love in Mission City Book 5)
Quinton's Quest (Love in Mission City Book 6)
Ulysses's Ultimatum (Love in Mission City Book 7)
Love in Mission City: The Boyfriend Gamble
Love in Mission City: The Four Seasons
Love in Mission City: The Boyfriends Duet
Love in Mission City: The Wedding Duet
Love in Mission City: The Shorts
Rayne Check
Archer's Awakening
Leo's Lust
Finn's Find
Pride Puppy
A Daddy for Christmas 3: Lorcan
Pup, Pup, and Away
A Daddy for Christmas 4: Raphael
Thought You Were the One
Love Without Reservations
Page Against the Machine
The Lightkeeper's Love Affair
Ace's Place
Marcus's Cadence
Not in it for the Money

Also:

Axe to Grind (Road to Rocktoberfest 2023)
Grindstone's Edge (Road to Rocktoberfest 2024)

Voice to Raise (Road to Rocktoberfest 2025)

Drums and Lullabies (Road to Rocktoberfest 2026)

Hugh (Single Dads of Gaynor Beach)

Anthony (Single Dads of Gaynor Beach)

Xavier (Single Dads of Gaynor Beach)

Love Furever (Friends of Gaynor Beach Animal Rescue)

Husky Love (Friends of Gaynor Beach Animal Rescue)

Yorkie to My Heart (Friends of Gaynor Beach Animal Rescue)

A Furever Home (co-written with Kaje Harper – Friends of Gaynor Beach Animal Rescue)

My Past, Your Future

If Only for Today

Catch a Tiger by the Tail

Solstice Surprise

Valentino in Vancouver

You See Me

Sun, Surf, and Surprises

Ginger in the City

Caressa's Homecoming (Bound by Love Book 1)

Cole's Reckoning (Bound by Love Book 2)

An Uncommon Gentleman

A Sensible Gentleman

A Wounded Gentleman

Didn't See You Coming

Finding Noah (Foggy Basin Season 2)

Noah's Holiday (A Foggy Basin Short Story)

Dancing Through Pride (A Foggy Basin Short Story)

Keystrokes and Kittens (Foggy Basin Season 3)

Hot Rucking Canadian

Big Rucking Disaster

Unlocked and Unlost

Audiobooks

Ginger Snapping All the Way

Stanley's Christmas Redemption

Sleigh Bells and Second Chances

Rayne's Return

Gideon's Gratitude

Quinton's Quest

Rayne Check

Archer's Awakening

Leo's Lust

Finn's Find

A Daddy for Christmas 2: Foster

A Daddy for Christmas 3: Lorcan

Puppy Pride

Thought You Were the One

Love in Mission City: The Shorts

Page Against the Machine

The Lightkeeper's Love Affair

Ace's Place

Marcus's Cadence

Not in it for the Money

Hugh (Single Dads of Gaynor Beach)

Anthony (Single Dads of Gaynor Beach)

Love Furever (Friends of Gaynor Beach Animal Rescue)

Husky Love (Friends of Gaynor Beach Animal Rescue)

A Furever Home (co-written with Kaje Harper – Friends of Gaynor Beach Animal Rescue)

My Past, Your Future
If Only for Today
Catch a Tiger by the Tail
Solstice Surprise
An Uncommon Gentleman
A Sensible Gentleman
Didn't See You Coming

Want a free short story? The story is set in Gaynor Beach, California where there are plenty of single dads and puppy rescues! You can sign up for my newsletter so you can keep up with all the great stuff I'm doing as well as pictures of my own pooches, Ally and Finnegan.

Hemingway's Happy Day

Love contemporary MF romances? What's better than love in the beautiful Cedar Valley in British Columbia, Canada? Find small town romances with a touch of angst, a bit of heat, and a lot of heart...

The Absolution of Abigail Reardon (prequel)
The Luminosity of Loriana Harper (Book 1)
The Making of Marnie Jones (Book 2)
The Redemption of Remy St. Claire (Book 3)

Interested in knowing more about Gabbi?

Sign up for her newsletter
Follow her on Bookbub
Follow her on Instagram

USA Today Bestselling author Gabbi Grey lives in beautiful British Columbia where her fur baby chin-poo keeps her safe from the nasty neighborhood squirrels. Working for the government by day, she spends her early mornings writing contemporary, gay, sweet, and dark erotic BDSM romances. While she firmly believes in happy endings, she also believes in making her characters suffer before finding their true love. She also writes m/f romances as Gabbi Black and Gabbi Powell.

www.ingramcontent.com/pod-product-compliance
Lightning Source LLC
LaVergne TN
LVHW050936080826
845145LV00004B/1293

* 9 7 8 1 9 9 7 9 0 4 5 2 6 *